I0723051

Stumblebum Waytes

Other Titles by Glenn Carley from Rock's Mills Press

Good Enough from Here (2020)

Jimmy Crack Corn (2022)

The Long Story of Mount Pester (2023)*†

The Long Story of Mount Pootzah (2023)*†

The Complete Long Stories (2024)*†

The One about Stella: A Little Fish (2024)*‡

* For children
† Co-authored with Nicholas Carley
‡ Co-authored with Adriana Carley

Stumblebum Waytes

A novel by
Glenn Carley

Rock's Mills Press
Rock's Mills, Ontario • Oakville, Ontario
2024

Published by
Rock's Mills Press
www.rocksmillspress.com

Copyright © 2024 by Glenn Carley. All rights reserved. This book may not be reproduced, in whole or in part, without the written permission of the publisher.

This is a work of fiction. Names, characters, businesses, places, events, locales, and incidents are either the products of the author's imagination or used in a fictitious manner. Any resemblance to actual persons, living or dead, or actual events is purely coincidental.

Cover image: Henry George Hine's (1811–1895) "The Waits at Seven Dials" (1853) portrays a group of "Christmas waits" or street musicians, including a trombonist. Source: *Illustrated London News*, 1853.

For information about this title, including retail, adoption, and bulk orders as well as permissions requests, please contact the publisher at customer.service@rocksmillspress.com.

For Ted Carley

Waytes, Waits, Waites:
a band of street or rustic serenaders who play or sing at night
for small gratuities.

(Webster's Collegiate Dictionary, 5th edition)

"And let each one perform some part:
To fill with joy, the warrior's heart."

(from "When Johnny Comes Marching Home Again")

Harvest Moon

(In which Billy gathers his sheaves)

I

Billy Hornpipe appears along a river-road which traces the base of a hill on his right and separates the silver ribbon of water to his left. Fog slips over the waxy skin of cedars whose rusty sweat looks like the iron in dried blood. Chills cool the fever-moisture that shrouds his breast, his shoulders and the ridges of his ribs and spine. He walks to exercise, after all, and not to linger. Walking is good for Billy's heart, for, it seems, his heart takes an unexpected beating. He passes a Retirement Home. There are cars in the parking lot and one of them flashes red at intervals. The blinking is rhythmic in the night, soothing some might say, and the pulsing silence interrupts the suction-like hiss when a dump truck brakes and passes wind. It is an orchestration of humans and equipment. Billy hears the soft chatter of nurses by the entrance to the Home. A door swishes open. A breath of ammonia exhales and hitches a ride on a white cloud of nicotine. O geezis! Billy gives smoking up long ago, under strict orders from his wife who says he stinks; and his doctor who says he is lucky. Still, he murders an imaginary cigarette, in an urgent panic of craving. Billy has time on his hands, lots of time. He is retired: long enough to lose track of the days but not long enough to purge the guilt of doing nothing. He is smart enough to maintain a routine for routine draws current and current begets energy and energy stokes purpose and where there is purpose; there is a return to some sort of meaning. Billy is desperate for meaning. He calculates the math at intervals of mood.

The calculus is not a morbid math but a pragmatic calculus. If his Mum dies at 78 (minus three months, palliative) and his Old Man dies at 76 (minus 4 years heart attack + 3 years X 2 hearing aids) to the power of n, where n= "what's that you say you said?" then … what is the mean-time left-to-live, minus (–) his current age? The atomic clock ticks. Billy giggles. Admittedly, his hearing is shaky but he is not divorced. They don't crab each other much. He loves Mrs. Hornpipe and she loves him.

You see, Billy Hornpipe arrives specifically in the pre-dawn to observe the Harvest Moon. When he is little, before he becomes what he becomes, he 'admires the heavens.' He wishes to; but he does not become a scientist, or an astronomer or an astronaut. Nonetheless, he thinks a fellow should know his own cosmos. A fellow should know where he comes from; where he is; why he's there and where he goes: Master and commander of his own ship, lord over the gravity of tides: A fellow who worries-not about the far side of his horizon.

The sky is clear. This Harvest Moon is radiant umber—too bright to look at directly; yet he beholds the orb directly and taunts her wattage to divert the wonder in his eyes. He lowers his head and for a moment he sees nothing; like a conk on the head; the way white renders black invisible and puts silver stars in it. The experience reminds Billy of lying on his back, squinting directly into the bulb of an overhead lamp, especially with the hissing and blinking and smells, like ammonia. He senses an outrage of blood on the sheets. Something inside him repairs itself. Soon, darkness opens his pupils, a luminescence forms and his sight returns to the river-road. He senses movement up at the bend. His gaze scans the grey edges. A creature lopes towards him. At first, he thinks it is a black cat. It passes through a ray of moonlight and purifies itself. By its bushy tale and pointed ears, Billy now identifies it as a fox. Billy thinks it must be feral for it does not make-way or skitter up the hill and into the cedars. It trots directly for him.

The hairs on Billy's neck stiffen. A tingling sensation begins at the base of his neck and tightens the skin around his temples, his eyes and his jaw. A primordial surge explodes deep inside him.

Heat radiates out to his clenched fist. Billy realizes he is a hunter and not a gatherer: His is not a flight reaction: It is a find-the-nearest-mastodon-bone-and-crush-the-fox's-skull-in reaction.

Billy spares the fox and moves to the other side of the road. The fox's tongue hangs out. It trots by Billy, stops and then turns.

"Are you feral?" the fox asks.

"Why do you say that? Billy replies.

"You look pale in the rusty moonlight."

"I feel perfectly fine," Billy says.

"Are you retired?" asks the fox.

"Why do you ask?" Billy replies.

"Your eyes are lost. They have no purpose. Do you have a purpose?"

"Not yet," Billy admits. "I am between purposes. There is lots of time."

"Well then, have you rediscovered meaning?"

"Not yet," Billy says. He grows uncomfortable now.

"You have no idea what to be when you grow up, do you?" the Fox says.

"I never did," Billy replies honestly

"Follow me then," says the fox.

Billy Hornpipe turns and with the moon behind him, traces his way towards town. Periodically, the fox stops, looks and waits for him to catch up.

Far up the road is a streetlight. It glows like a spirit with outstretched arms. Billy spots the T-junction, sees the bridge to the right and traces the long road on the left that leads into town. He senses the moment and pauses. He feels the light of the Harvest Moon upon the back of his neck. The moon calls to him and her gravity makes him turn. Billy turns slowly, and by degrees, like the phases of the moon—there is no rush: waxing crescent, first quarter, waxing gibbous to face the full moon; but his body does not stop there. His rotation continues: waning gibbous, third quarter, waning crescent to face fully, the shiny grin of the new moon. Billy feels he is both re-winding and unwinding and the feeling is not unpleasant. Fever lightens the load. The crescent, quarters and slices of gibbous light offers a clear glimpse of his journey; of the way he came from childhood right up to the feeling of the pavement under the soles of his running shoes. It as if he is on the side of a mountain and looks back into a fertile valley, watered by rivers shepherded under a blue expanse. Across the distance Billy makes out no real detail, only clusters of forms: groves of oak trees, a boundary of vineyard, a silver ribbon of river and hills backed by white clouds on the horizons. A conical strip of Lebanon cedars stands at parade rest. Billy lingers at the memory while Mrs. Hornpipe and their children bustle at home in the sun. He smiles a smile of fullness and joy: By grace of elevation, he forgets details of any sense of loss.

'Enough gravity,' Billy says to himself. He turns his back on the Harvest Moon. He continues to follow the fox but the moon has a different idea. Billy's movement now is involuntary. He begins to turn again and not of his own accord: Slowly at first and then with increasing speed. The crescent, quarter and gibbous slivers of light spin like a calliope and the full and new moon now wink like a strobe.

"Behold the whirling dervish!" the feral fox cries from under the lamplight.

"It feels beautiful to lose control!" Billy cries out.

"You are ready now," the fox replies.

II

It is an odd thing but Billy does not feel dizzy when the spinning stops. He feels naked and not ashamed, but looks to reassure himself that his being is clothed. He is outside, after all. Modesty aside, Billy knows he is no longer a spring chicken is the honest way to tell it. He shrugs out a puff of breath and pats his tummy.

Billy Hornpipe lifts his eyes onto the asphalt stage of the lamp light. The fox is gone. He shifts his sightline to the left. In the umbra of the second street light, he sees the fox scamper and then turn. The creature's stare penetrates Billy's pupils. Billy's give as good as he gets: Their communion is complete.

He walks forward and turns left.

It is indeed, garbage day. Billy sees that a Picker pulls up beside other people's junk by the curb. He claims his territory in the neighbourhood yet respects the other rag-and-bones folks' turf on the south hill, the north hill, down by the river and out towards the sawmill-ruins where the town looks nice and cozies up to corn fields. This Picker cleverly conceals his pick-up truck in the shadows outside of the glow of the street light. The engine runs. The driver-side door shuts with a clunk. The man emerges from around the front of the truck, mounts the sidewalk, makes his inspection and lifts a drum with straps on it, tenderly, into a space behind the cab. Billy strides forward. He says good morning and takes his measure of the fellow. He notices that the man is tall and that his waistline is good. A black sweatshirt makes his white hair look even whiter. In the gray-time before the gossamer light of day-sky, the man ages well. Expertly, he returns to the sidewalk and gathers copper pipe like pick-up sticks. They ring beautifully when he slides them into the trailer attached to a hitch on his truck. 'What a sonorous splash of notes', Billy thinks to himself.

"What is your name?" Billy asks the man.

"Slim Picker and yours?"

"Billy Hornpipe," Billy replies.

"Have you been retired for a while now, Slim Picker?" Billy asks cordially.

"Yes, I have. How can you tell?"

"There is purpose in your eyes and meaning in your step," the red fox interjects.

Slim Picker shrugs his shoulders. "It's a hobby, I guess." He looks at Billy and points his finger. "Is the critter yours?"

The question makes Billy nervous.

"Yes, he is," Billy declares. "You can't have him, he's … my conscience."

"You talk to yourself, then?" Slim asks.

"Doesn't everyone?" Billy replies.

The fox pokes his nose into the rubble and sniffs. A plastic shovel slides off. Underneath it, a small horn glimmers in the Harvest Moon. It has a reed on the tip and a bell on one end.

"Nice find!" says the Picker.

"May I have it?" Billy asks.

"Only if you know how to play it. It's called a shawm. In olden times, watchmen play it to mark time and let the village know they are on duty and not sleeping."

"Yes, I can play it," Billy lies. "I was in the high school band, the pit orchestra, a recorder consort and a garage band. I let it all go across time for some reason. How hard can it be?"

Billy licks his fingers with saliva. He rubs the reed and dries it off with a twist of his shirt. He moistens the reed with his tongue, inhales and purses his lips like a prune. A loud, piercing whine wakes up a dozen birds.

"This is perfect," Billy cries. "I feel like a snake charmer!"

"Take the instrument, Brother, but leave the rest of the piles to me," Slim Picker generously offers. When you retire it is important to get back to the things you love. I love to keep moving. The garbage truck will be along soon."

"Thank you, Slim Picker. It is a pleasure to meet you," Billy calls out.

A truck door slams, a gear groans and the pick-up lurches forward. The trailer waddles obediently; content, the way a dog wags its tail. "Same time next week!" Slim Picker calls back. The drum with the strap rolls and makes a sonorous hollow sound when it wobbles into place in the bed of Slim's pick-up truck.

For a moment, Billy feels like there is purpose in his eye but it is just a piece of grit.

The red fox stops. She sniffs the air. The Harvest Moon changes colour. A red rind of dawn dilutes the blackness.

Billy clutches the shawm. "Maybe I'll be a watchman when I grow up."

"Stay with me," the fox says. She trots forward along the long road into town.

Billy lifts his gaze. On the other curb of the long road that leads into town, he beholds another pile of domestic junk. Slim monitors one side of the street at a time and this allows him to focus quickly and methodically. Billy observes that the new heap of nothing is unsullied. The red fox narrows her eyes in warning.

"Don't be selfish, Billy. Get outside yourself. You won't be sick forever."

Billy Hornpipe feels vaguely irked at the accusation. He thinks of Mrs. Hornpipe.

Billy crosses the road. In-betwixt and in-between the flotsam of recovery, Billy spies the glint-and-glimmer of a valve trombone. He moves a greasy oven rack, pries out a broken vacuum cleaner and frees the brassy instrument. The slide moves perfectly like a liquid thing. He tries the valves, hoists the horn, strokes the slide and points it up at the Harvest Moon.

"Behold Gretchen Moncur III," he laughs. "Jack Teagarden. Me and Curtis Fuller." Billy notes that the mouthpiece is intact but the bell has a dent in it—a little love tap.

"Achtung! Who goes there?" a womanly-voice declares in the twilight.

"I am Billy Hornpipe," Billy replies sheepishly. "I am out for a walk and this is my fox, Turnip."

"Did he fall off a truck?"

"No, he is smarter than he looks," Billy explains. "May I have the trombone?"

"Why?" asks the woman.

"I am not sure," Billy says.

"Well, take it then," the woman laughs. "Perhaps it serves a purpose."

"Are you retired?" Billy wonders.

"I am close … and very ready," the woman says wistfully. "What makes you ask?"

"It is in your eyes," Billy replies. "I see purpose still. It's all around you. I hear meaning in your voice. Are you spiritual? What is your name?"

"My friends call me Straw. We are of the Germanic Tribe and we are very good musicians. My name means Straw in your language. I am the last of the straws."

"Are you the long straw or the short straw," Billy politely asks.

"Both," the woman laughs.

"I am lucky to meet you," Billy smiles. "Do you play valve trombone?"

"Yes, but other instruments interest me now. I play everything, but I prefer the euphonium. I cart a cello around or a violin, once and a while, when I feel a spring in my step. I am busy now but I hope to play more."

"Why do you put off playing?" Billy asks.

"Who knows?" Straw replies. "If you'll pardon me, I must go now and tend to my burn-barrel."

Billy smells the funky maple aroma of tree limb and leaf smoke. Straw retreats down her laneway into a back yard.

"You can come and watch if you like," she says.

The fox waits at the curb. Shyly, Billy walks down the driveway. He steps onto the apron of a patio that opens to the back yard. Billy sees a fifty-gallon drum with holes in it. It stands on cement blocks in the centre of the yard. A fire roars within and sends beautiful licks of red, yellow and blue sparks skyward, into a suggestion of light.

Straw turns. She laughs like a wind in chimes. Her tintinnabulation is lovely.

"It is my own design!" she exclaims.

"Why do you do this?" Billy wonders.

"I love to burn things, in my yard, from my neighbour's yards, from the park down by the silver ribbon of river, and they say, smoke is like a prayer.

"What do you pray for?"

"More wood," Straw laughs.

Turnip whines and gives Billy the high sign.

"It is a pleasure to meet you," Billy says. "I must continue my walk with the fox. Perhaps we will run into one another again. I shall bring you wood! I know a man with a pick-up and a trailer, too!"

"I'm not going anywhere. See you around!" says a wind in the chimes.

III

Billy sees that the street lights will be laid-off soon and on the dole for the rest of the day. Sunshine sweeps her way across the valley, so eager to punch the solar clock. Reluctantly, the Harvest Moon blends into nothing. Turnip rubs against the side of Billy's leg. He looks down and the fox trots onward towards the T-junction that separates the long road by the river from a main road that slices through town like a stripe on a skunk. Billy raises his head and traces the path of the fox. Under a wavering lamplight, Billy beholds two men standing on a bridge. He recognizes them both, not because he knows them but because he often sees them in the village. In fact; Billy sees them so much that he bestows names upon them—a common practice in the so-called Village of Blight. Running Horse is a boy with long hair who finds it impossible to walk. He gallops wild and free, through the core and up main drag to the South Hill. His carefree youth becomes him.

Old Stilt walks with a limp and sucks constantly on a blade of grass. Billy hears him get a good shriek out of it when he forms a reed between his thumbs. Stilt works at the pharmacy Billy frequents, now.

"Don't forget to take your pills," Mrs. Hornpipe calls out.

Billy ignores Mrs. Hornpipe. He watches Grizelda, the Negativity Cleanser. She works in the fortune-telling shop off the main drag. The thin digital sign disorients Billy, with its horizontal red letters that flow from right to left: Palms Read…. Fortunes Told…. Tarot Cards…. Ear Candling…. Negativity Cleansing…. Money Taken…. (Repeat to infinity).

"I got you a Negativity Cleansing gift-card for your birthday Sweetie."

"I'd rather have my palms read," Billy whispers.

Billy Hornpipe approaches the two men chatting on the Bridge. He sees it is Lord Bogroll and The Yeti. Yeti presents well, as a man of small stature and generous laugh. His long white hair and a mostly-white beard creates an elegant look. Billy knows The Yeti drinks Real-Ale at the Neam; a pub in the 'Village of Blight' that retired souls frequent. His stomach growls: Yeti eats French fries or mushy peas when he feels lonely. Three-in-the-afternoon bores the hell out of Yeti and the Neam fills certain retired time and half-empty space with foam. Billy guffaws every time he overhears Yeti says 'village.' On the historic blue plaque that greets strangers at the gate, or welcomes bedroom-community commuters' home from the city, a ne'er-do-well spray paints a Black B over the white V-in-Village. Delinquency is relentless and despite efforts by the Mayor, the Region gives up painting over the B "since 1992." (Welcome to the *Billage of Blight*, founded 1872, population 14,100.) The town thinks the sign is a real knee-slapper.

Billy often sees The Yeti roam the parking lot across the road from the Neam, en route for soft ice cream in the afternoons. This proves his soul is retired. Purpose in his step and meaning in his eye guides all movement and promotes Yeti as Veteran of the Atomic Clock., a shape-shifter, not a hand-wringer; equal parts Sasquatch, Big Foot or Snow-Man, Abominable.

Meanwhile, back at the bridge, Billy sees Yeti clutch a trumpet in his hand and clap Lord Bogroll on the back. His eyes twinkle. He puffs his cheeks and sounds off a mischievous morning *blat* on the instrument. A reveille of sorts, like a … like a … like a Watchman! Billy laughs at the insight. One at a time each retired man turns to say hello to Billy.

Lord Bogroll knows he has a good gig. He waters the town flowers in boxes along the bridge rails; draped on high, like earrings on lamp posts, while brown urns blossom on every street corner, in the Merry Olde Billage of Blight. Aside from the fact that his flowers look healthy, the gift of Lord Bogroll's gig is that he drives a golf cart which pulls a tiny trailer that carries a large white drum of water. It slooshes when Lord B glides by. Billy thinks *a sloosh* is a beautiful note. He sees Lord Bogroll most days on his walks and for all the world, the man's activity resembles a bee on-the-job. The golf cart glides silently and stops. A wand reaches to the sky and soon a cascade of water spatters the cool cement. Each flower grows red and purple and happy. Like pollination, the golf cart flits to the next pot, the one after that and so on. From experience, Billy sees that Lord Bogroll is at the end of his route. This is why he slows time and chats with Yeti. Bogroll masters the casual call and response of retired time. The way he works so hard, though, makes Billy suspicious of the man; until he overhears a woman at the bakery call *the Flower Guy,* lucky to be retired. After that, Billy greets the good Lord B cheerily, whenever his golf cart glides by and sunrise announces the end of his shift.

In the dark, when the dew still saturates the air, Billy chats with Lord Bogroll. Turns out he is from Belize—head gardener on a resort. He knows a lot about the moon, too. He says moons are bigger and brighter where he comes from. "Brighter than my wife's smile!"

Today, by chance, it pleases Billy to approach the two men. He hopes to get to know The Yeti. Turnip scampers slightly out-of-view behind a blue garbage drum. A clarinet pokes out of a bag on the back seat of the golf cart.

Lord Bogroll must be a Picker too, Billy notes. Up close, he sees that the two men's eyes look amused and inviting; they twinkle at no man's expense, the way experience passes through the hub-bub and rigmarole of life and learns to feel comfortable in its own skin.

"You haven't been retired long, have you?" asks Yeti.

"My eyes give it away," Billy concedes.

"Give them time," Lord Bogroll grins like a jack-o-lantern innerlit with purpose. "Where did you get the shawm? Do you play?"

"No," Billy replies.

"Well give that time too, Chum," Yeti replies. "There is no time like *dat, dat and datly-dat* on the snare of pleasant aimlessness."

Lord Bogroll steps on the accelerator, does a sharp U-turn and silently glides away.

"It is a pleasure to meet you!" Billy calls out.

The Billage bustles now. The timeless ordeal of 'follow the leader' starts an urgent game of commute. The convoy points directly to the heart of a citified southern horizon; where a conga-line of grid-locked high-rises shimmies, mocks and waves. A grocery truck grinds her gears. Exhaust plumes the air. The Yeti says good morning and turns. He makes his way to the Billage coffee shop with all the time in the world. At silly intervals he blats his trumpet. The cluster of notes creates a mischievous effect. Like it or not, Billy compares the sound to metallic farts that smell like diesel.

"Well. Have you learned anything?" the fox asks.

"Maybe," Billy Hornpipe replies.

"I taught you everything I know and still you're feral?"

"Try again tomorrow?" Billy wonders, sheepishly and shrugs his shoulders.

"Practice your shawm," the fox orders. She leaves via a side-yard to follow the patchwork-scent of back-yards to the silver ribbon of river.

Billy goes home and worries about getting bored again.

Blue Moon

("… you saw me standin' alone, without a dream in my heart,
without a love of my own…")

I

Billy Hornpipe sleeps at home. He imagines a sexy torch-singer in a white mermaid dress. He hears a nostalgic song in a softly-lit nightclub, but forgets the lyrics. Perhaps days go by, but there is no time and space—only pictures painted by languid thoughts, vividly so. He passes through a world of stained glass. Each fragment is indifferent, bounded by lead: Each piece patches together to form sensations of meaning that transform into other meanings and new fragments: As quickly as they appear, they disappear. Billy tries to understand but he does not understand. He senses the gentle rise and fall of his chest. An unruly finger twitches. When warmth replaces chill, he submerges into a deeper reality where nothing hisses and nothing beeps—a place of glorious Technicolor with no intrusions of sound.

Billy Hornpipe beholds a primordial green forest on the west coast whose trees he sees but cannot identify. It is the same with red flowers. It is the same with blue-bottle insects. He observes a massive grey slug, five inches long—a prehistoric thing. Billy prepares, as if to race. The cross-country course takes him through the provinces, first over the mountains, along the silver rivers, through the flatlands, around Igneous Inuksuk-besotted monuments, to finish at the Billage of Blight. At a house on a mountain, a little girl brings him flowers. She wishes to run with Billy but Billy runs faster. A chime of laughter twinkles in his wake. It surprises him, the way colourized sound makes dreams more animate than silent. A rope ladder appears. Billy tests the tight rungs with the palms of his hands. He clutches the bulbs of knots and strains his neck to look up. The ladder ascends through the base of a cloud. Billy feels his density of self. He worries about the sheer ordeal of ascension for his carcass is gravity bound. He wishes his waistline was flat. The atomic clock ticks. The race is on. He climbs, one rung at a time. Billy's lightness surprises him and before long he feels first wet-wisps, the soft gauze of cloud, like a damp pillow, moistened by sweat and errant spittle. Billy feels light inside his eyelids. He opens his eyes and gazes into the splendour of a Blue Moon. Her light exceeds the umber of the Harvest Moon and her glow prophesizes a coldness to come; perhaps an anticipated pre-warmth of morning. Yet on the road, beside the cedars on his left and the silver ribbon of river on the right, Billy feels content. He lifts his arms in an arc behind his back and his stretch resolves all tension: from instep to forearm, from cartilage to joint and he feels whole, again.

"Welcome back," the red fox says.

"Who are you again?" Billy replies, bewildered.

"Turnip, your fox," the fox answers.

"Why do I call you Turnip?"

"Because I am smarter than you look," the fox smiles. "Follow me."

Billy reluctantly turns his back on the Blue Moon. He follows Turnip. She trots with resolve towards the T-junction where the long road leads left into town. A tell-tale tug of gravity slows Billy Hornpipe's sense of urgency. Like it or not, but mostly liking it, Billy turns and lifts his face feverishly, into the fullness of the Blue Moon. There is complete communion. Crescent, quarter, gibbous slivers of light beget a full illumination, which swirls swiftly, then reverses to waning gibbous, quarter and crescent lunar-blinks of strobe. The new moon smiles upon Billy. It is a dervish now, faster and faster, whirs and blurs and the darkness gives way to a screen of light whose shafts lift Billy upward, like thieves at Golgotha; and then, his light solidifies, to become an elevated firmness of ground.

Billy is at the bridge. Behind him, the North Hill and the road out of town; before him, the skunk-stripe that is the main drag of the Billage of Blight. It leads up the South Hill to the outskirts. Billy feels profoundly grey and unhealthy.

"Are we flying?" Billy asks.

"We are not," the red fox replies.

Billy's eyes widen. "Elevation is not a bad thing...." he says in awe.... "But what is the purpose?"

"There are some things I want to show you," the fox answers. "Come."

Billy takes a tentative step, perceives the firmness of step and turns south, to head into town.

II

Ascendency offers insight and Billy Hornpipe takes a meta-view of the Billage of Blight. He sees quantum details amidst the Big-Bang of it all. He sees his life below him: the scatter of buildings, their relationships to one another, the randomness of construction and the urgent claim upon every square inch: Views of after-thought, of greed, land-lust and violation; one or two spaces of beauty whose isolation suggests at best an oasis and at worst a space that cowers beside a siege of inherited ugliness. Blight is an old spirit grown feral with clusters of scabs on its arms and its legs. It means well; but a momentum overtakes it, as if to say, Blight and every other Billage where the city infects the country, can't help what happens to it. Her prophesy was foretold decades ago by visionaries who profit from the urban script of growth.... Developers and fast-thinkers that move away or pass away before their calamity takes root.

"My God, the Billage looks like me, on a bad day," Billy thinks to himself.

"You have time to think now," says the Fox.

"Is that a good thing?" Billy asks.

"Yes," replies the fox.

"I have been reckless," Billy confesses.

Turnip speaks a greater truth. In his other life, Billy remembers the hubbub and malarkey of decades of velocity; a career well-served and a salary well-spent; a life in the currents. It all flies by so fast, like the phenomenon of houses taken for granted on a daily commute. He sees and he does not see. He sees what he recognizes. He does not see what he does not recognize. He misses vivid moments that exist amidst the blur; like the house with the hedge, the Victorian turrets by the Church, the Monster home whose shade robs the neighbour's tomato garden of all life and then suddenly, on a Tuesday or a Sunday, Billy sees a house that for his entire life, he completely missed. He senses an invisible visibility—a Stumble-bum reality that exists somewhere between space and time.

"It is good to think! Even if I don't know what to do with the thoughts," Billy confesses.

"About time," chuckles Billy's Fox.

"How much beauty have I actually missed?"

Kin to *terra firma*, the *fortis lux* rays of Blue Moon that he walks upon inform Billy's visions. The light forces him not to rush. Methodically, he surveys the main drag of the Billage of Blight. The road now looks more like a frayed black belt from a thrift shop than a skunk-stripe. Billy notes a series of hand-crafted extra holes puncture the tip of the belt. Absentmindedly, he pulls his track pants up. His gaze meets each subject before him, as if for the first time. The Bridge, where he stands, spans the river: It is one of three crossroads. Behind him the North Hill distances itself from the creep of subdivision. A land of silos, green and blue tractors takes shape: red barns, corn, corn and more corn. The sound of hammer and nails ceases here, for this land claims its watershed: It will not be bought off: The people listen. Billy likes to drive north with Mrs. Hornpipe and a coffee-after-dinner to watch deer-at-dusk. Corn, corn, corn grows to the West. A flock of sheep and a herd of cattle hold the ground. Little do they know that a six-lane highways plots murder next year. "It'll git some Wetland, too," *sez* the farmers. Frogs and red-wing blackbirds already sound the alarm. A painted turtle inches her way north. The creature sidesteps the flattened pancake of a squished brother, picked clean by crows. Billy swerves to look east: A "Now Trending" developer's sign plants itself arrogantly, smack-dab in a fallow field. The sign boasts: houses, houses, houses, condos, condos, condos as the new urban corn. Billy blames the Billage next to Blight for the onslaught. Any Old timer knows that the grass, the gardens and the trees of Serenity Acres, soaks in the saturate-spew of dismantled auto wrecking yards; where eager children will one day, treasure-hunt for starter motors, shiny brake pads and headlights.

With only a germ of a purpose; *without a love of his own*, Billy gazes south, up the main drag and sees it for the first time. Parts of him honestly do not care. He glides forward: neither wraith, nor good spirit, just Billy and his fox.

III

The street below Billy Hornpipe bustles and dithers: Behold the fanfare for the common man!

Billy spots The Yeti as he lopes towards the coffee shop. It is not jealousy but admiration, he feels, for ritual is a glorification of routine, a fixed necessity, a must-do injection of intention in the space and time present in each day; perhaps, a sweet honey-bun knot in the golden ascension of Providence. The caffeine 'don't hurt' and Billy wants to murder a black coffee. At precise intervals, The Abominable One raises his golden trumpet like Gabriel and blats out notes on his atomic clock: Alarmed, a passerby jaywalks to avoid collision. Billy smiles at the bearded watchman. His make-believe effort reveals the exquisite reality within a sea of nothing. Billy inhales: He purses his lips, blows into his shawm and sends a wonderfully whine-y response to Yeti's call. Yeti stops, looks around but neglects to look up. An aroma overpowers and as if by tidal pull, sweeps Yeti into the coffee shop. Billy watches a well-dressed lawyerly-looking fellow, as he strides north, past a variety store which boasts a menagerie of coloured glass bongs, hydra-armed hookahs and stone hash pipes: a treasure trove that tempts those within walking distance of the Billage high school. The proprietor pulls the deaf, dumb and blind card when a Retiremento stops to give him the gears for selling hallucinogens. His fox waits patiently by the curb. By an act of poetic justice, the creature relieves itself on the lamp post in front of the store. Suddenly, Billy discovers the difference between the worker-bees and the Re-tirementos. Congregated over by the bench; assembled reverently around the Cenotaph in the square; or in front of historic plaques that tell the true story of each building on the main drag; Billy sees a Retiremento takes not-a-thing for granted; for not only does he have time to think, he takes time to wonder. There lies the rub. At elevation, Billy Hornpipe pauses to take inventory. He sweeps his eyes from the top of the east side of the main drag, across the bridge behind him and up the main drag, to the top of the west side which bisects a second crossroads at the four corners. Not to be fooled by cheap imitations, Billy's eyes hammer the ersatz commerce streetscape like pop-ups at an arcade.

An opportunistic building poaches the ancient hardware store, strips it of its history and calls the first of two tattoo shops: *Your Body/My Canvas*. Across the road, on the top floor, Queequeg's Magical Ink (QMI?) robs and replaces a landmark bank. The nail shop, the mortgage and loan, the garish coffee boutique overrun a Post Office, a farm co-op and a saddle shop, respectively. Every elementary teacher in every school petitions Blight's Bizness Association to insist upon standardized spelling. A Ward Councillor promises results in the spring election: It will be death to *Peet's Peatzah, Bi-rite@ Di Wel.com* and *Samz Sammeez* when students fail quizzes in droves. Billy wonders if nothing is important anymore or if everything is.

He panics. By the light of the Blue Moon, Billy inspects his wardrobe: cheesy running shoes, velour sweat pants that sag at the bum, favourite T-shirt-with-hole-under-an-arm, faded oversized sweatshirt to hide errant man-teats and undies he wears for three days. And there it is: No ties, no dresses, no slacks, no dress shirts; only ratty cardigans, hole-y jeans, stretch-pants and sweat-stuff with hockey logos or forgotten universities. The sorting completes itself. Billy recognizes exactly who is who on the main drag below, and he gravitates to those who walk with foxes. He brushes out a wrinkle on his track pants.

"It's really not a bad look on you," Turnip says agreeably,

Billy startles, tilts his head and gazes down, lost in thought.

"Are we flying?" he asks, again.

"No just absorbing," the red fox, replies.

"Do I have a fever?" Billy asks.

"Yes," the fox replies.

"Am I changing?" Billy whispers.

"You'll always be my spring chicken," Mrs. Hornpipe says, tenderly.

"Keep looking," orders the fox.

Just then, Straw emerges from the old River Pub by the bridge. Billy notices the pub is under new management for the fifteenth time. A spider-y *sine-on-a-stand* with blocked phlorescent alphabet letters cries out like the Billage beggar, to all who listen: NEW LOOK! NEW BEER! NEW ME. THIS TIME I GET THE KUR-RI RITE! 10 PER ##@$$% OFF. To Billy, the squatty signs perch Raven-like, everywhere at street level; each one a tiny wannabe billboard that obstructs clear views for left turns into traffic. Straw steps with resolve. She disappears behind the derelict Mortgage & Loan building and emerges onto a stone patio. The patio connects a dead roadhouse with a multi-purpose bistro that outlives the corpse. The Obsessa boasts a fresh coat of paint. Like blood on a sheet, a neon Help Wanted sign stains a white background. Billy senses the want-ad is a posting to eternity. He knows The Obsessa doesn't really know what kind of store she is. He remembers she used to be the site of Vinnies Best Beal in Town. Above her, a pool hall constantly breaks even but now progress kicks both businesses to the curb in piles of plaster, rogue-nails and wood. Everyone anticipates the next fine dining in Blight: UNDER RENNOVATION. COMING SOON.

"Somebody hang *that* sign around my neck," Billy guffaws.

Straw stops. She gazes through a window and nods her head. Purposely she turns, crosses the patio and collects scraps of wood from a blue bin that peaks around the corner from the back of the Obsessa. Later, an air current sweeps the funky smoke of oak two-by-fours that scent the wind. She is at her burn-barrel again.

A kerfuffle erupts at the cross roads: The road with the street that leads east to Serenity Acres or shoots west, to the six-lane crime scene in-waiting: where concrete meets corn-field and kicks its arse. Billy sees Lord Bogroll. He finishes his watering. The light awakens the sky. The Blue Moon fades. Bogroll demonstrates his other purpose in Retiremento life: Eighteen-wheel trucks make illicit right turns at the corner; or blow northward, straight through the Billage. Lord Bogroll knows he must stop them. After all; a sign warns these *nogoodniks* repeatedly, to use the by-pass around, not through, the Billage. Their vibration causes flower petals to flutter onto the side-walk. Righteously, the good Lord B yells at the truckers. Perhaps in Belize he was a cop but in the Billage, he takes it upon himself to be *Tiananmen Boggy*. A rig honks its mighty horn, releases its Jake brake, lurches forward and crawls. Tiananmen Boggy shuffles to block it. Everyone gathers to watch the show down. The jerky choreography continues until the Doppler effect of siren arrives well before the red-blue wink of flashing lights. Tiananmen Bogroll relents-not. The trucker puts his rig in gear, spews diesel, and lumbers stupidly forward. Like a machine with loose bowels, the truck growls and waddles northerly, towards the Wetlands, to flatten snakes and turtles into road-kill as pay-back. Everyone loves dear Lord Bogmiester for his efforts to beautify Blight and keep her safe.

He mounts his golf cart, hefts his clarinet, blows a victory-cadenza, and then silently glides away around the corner of an empty building that once sold fish.

"I am exhausted," Billy sighs. "My body aches. The *fortis lux* is spongy at my feet."

"Go home and rest," advises the red fox.

"Are you sure you won't abandon me?" Billy asks.

"We will complete your survey tomorrow," replies the fox.

Billy rolls under the covers. The exertion makes him sweat. He hears sounds of euphonium, of valve trombone, drum, trumpet and shawm. Charmed, a snake pops the lid off a basket. It hisses at him and slithers through the crack of a wide door. A flashing red light chases a truck. He hears no sound. Billy sees glass fragments stitched with lead. He grasps a last moment of lucidity before he sinks into the swirl of his dervish. Billy Hornpipe realizes he is all dressed down, with nowhere to go.

IV

The First Micro Moon

He fights it at first, but gravity once again takes hold. Billy Horn-pipe swishes and flutters like a quarter on its way down through aqueous space, destined but in no rush to rest on a sea-bed. The full Blue Moon recedes. She grows tiny and distant in the black expanse above and twinkles like a pin prick or the eyes of a Yeti.

Like a thermocline at depth, a wave of anxiety overwhelms Billy and he shivers. He stops sinking and finds himself in a familiar place that recurs constantly now. Billy Hornpipe commutes to work and rejoins the conga-line. He officially leaves 'a year ago' but for some reason returns. A colleague stops on the stairs and says hello on her way to the cafeteria. She seeks, nay lusts after a black coffee. As if he never left, Billy works pro bono now, but he is stranded in the lobby. He remembers his phone (land line), his desk and his assistant are all upstairs. He goes upstairs and can only look in through a window to the inner space. A colleague approaches his office door. Billy interprets all the gestures, knows what to say but his television-is-on-mute now. The silence deafens. Billy descends to the lobby. He discovers a small cubicle, with a desk and a window. A pen lolls on his desk. It waits to be used. Turnip-the-fox curls up on a soft green blotter in the sun and gazes outside. Billy names her Tulip now.

"Do you see the Lebanon Cedars in the field?" Tulip asks.

"Do you see the silver ribbon of the river?

"Do you see the vineyard?"

"I do," replies Billy. "Why do I call you Tulip now?"

"You are transforming," says the fox.

Billy reaches for and then sees that there is no phone inside his cubicle. He sees there is no desktop computer so he cannot return emails. There is nothing to write on and his pen goes to waste. Another colleague stops by for an opinion, the way they always do. Billy panics. It rubs his ethic to give advice when he is pro bono and really not even there. He does not want a lawsuit to take his house.

'All my relationships are changing,' Billy Hornpipe whispers. 'I no longer relate to those who actually work, talk about work or grouse about work. It is odd. I have no place. My old life is a pin-prick; like how a valley looks from the side of a mountain. There is too much distance.'

Tulip empathizes with his thoughts: "You are tired of commuting too."

"2 (hours a day) X 5 (days a week) = 10 hours (to the power of n) where n = a sixth unpaid day," Billy moans, and quotes his calculus, as if by rote.

"Give yourself an 'A', Billy. This is why you walk in the moon-light," Tulip offers. "It is why Slim scrounges, Lord Bogroll rides his golf cart, Yeti lopes and Straw burns wood."

"Do they fill a vacuum?" Billy wonders.

"Velocity creates suction," replies the fox.

"Did I get hurt? Do I have post-traumatic stress? Why am I so cranky?"

"Who knows? Ask your wife…." Tulip says and then disappears.

The thermocline releases Billy from her ice-y grip. He flutters upward. The sea-bed sinks out of view. Gentle flutters of ascension are not unpleasant.

The micro-moon draws near, larger now. Her luminescence casts shadows. Billy feels his pillow, moist, against both cheeks. He rocks his head like a dervish out-of-gear; like a Jake-brake on a rig, unable to whirl yet needing to whirl. When he opens his eyes, Billy senses the soft paste of instant mash potatoes, the weak aroma of coffee and the viscous syrup of fruit cocktail. 'Yuck,' he thinks.

V

"Sorry I'm late," Billy says to Tulip. "The Blue Moon is still out. How can this be?

"You were not gone long," says the fox.

Billy Hornpipe returns to the bustle and dither of the main drag below. Behold the bedroom community! The south hill rises steeply. A temporary fireworks store pops-up on his left. A wob-bly cartoon flagstaff flutters Big Bangs and Welcomes: (CC: Cash only). On the right, the Exceptional Women's Dress store rises like a phoenix upon the ashes of annual foreclosures. A box store clutches the hips of a strip mall and everything is online, anyway. Peet's Peatzah surrenders his him/her/it monopoly. Billy loses count of garish sub-shops, wrap and Billage-burger joints: Grease bubbles on the land that keeps food hot after the long commute: (CC: Buy local).

An older subdivision blossoms at the top of the hill and the trees look nicer. A clatter of debris catches Billy's ear. Slim Picker makes his wobbly rounds, trailer-in-tow. His routine marks the day. It is Monday. The Retirementos all have a reference point: Tomorrow is Tuesday the way a grocery flier tells it. Billy smiles at Lord Bogroll, man among men, as he glides south, bee-like with purposeful intent. He pollinates yellow marigold, purple petunia, white snapdragon and green vine with water. It feels beautiful until Billy notices an outrage of graffiti on the wall behind the gardener: Hieroglyphics of lust and profanity: An ape's rendition of balls and penis-on-wall, ad nauseum: Again? Youth? Really? C'mon … who raised these testosterone-besotted cretins? A miracle mile on the right competes with the miracle mile on the left, locked together like bull walruses in a life-or-death struggle for the territorial rights of concrete.

Again, the scabies of Blight is her developers and her near-sighted deal-makers, voted in. Money, money, money is the corn, corn, corn of Billage sprawl: A mad soul sinks a chain-link fence into the parking lot. Set in cement, defiant, it protests and bisects and separates the land someone owns from the land someone wants. The barrier renders an entire swath of retail stores without access to anyone, really. Soon, the lights flicker, the pavement cracks, mortar falls out in chinks and then in the hard-rain of commerce, a disintegration of bricks. No longer Worker-bee, or Retiremento, the hapless *disgruntlese* are *shit-out-of-work and shit-out-of-luck*. Billy resents the random robberies of greed but also notes there, but for grace of us; a pension is a lovesome thing.

"I really am a lucky sap, aren't I?" Billy says.

"Seems that way," the fox replies.

"Mrs. Hornpipe and I put some thought into it, you know."

"Scrimp and save is a lost art and luck, the currency of fore-sight," says Tulip.

"Do I whine too much, Tulip?"

"Perhaps," replies the red fox.

A breeze shifts Billy for a moment to the west.

VI

Billy Hornpipe observes the suburban landscape. He is west of the main drag of Blight. He plants his feet firmly on *fortis lux*—the strong light. Blue moonlight magnifies and where there is magni-fication, an inner meaning reveals itself but only to those who wish to see. To see is to perceive and to perceive, sparks all kindling of meaning, tentative at first and then in the flames of resolve, the fire takes hold, builds, spreads and rises—any burn barrel knows that. Tulip trots alongside, Billy but perhaps not for long.

Billy sees countless souls walking dogs. Domesticity is in the air, almost like canine dander: A man and a woman, two wom-en, two men, a boy, a girl. An old soul in velour picks his way along a cattle trail to his water. His fox is beside him. A gray-haired woman in *senstible* shoes and stretch pants heads in the opposite direction. Her rump is self-aware, round and becoming. Her fox chats intently with another fox. A mother pushes a stroller while the family pup sniffs and wanders, wanders and sniffs. Each mutt senses the scent of life; the urgency of it, the have-to discoveries, and the gnawing resolution to find whatever this feral thing is, in the air. Billy does too. He laughs at the plump blue baggies, clev-erly tied to leashes. He smells the stink of discard: The responsible removal of street-beef by one and all frankly makes him gag. Billy is not a fan of dawgs.

Billy beholds a patchwork of back yards, the personality of place within the clutter of space: a pool, a large deck with a bar-becue and a fish-smoker; a cacophony of junk, saved boards, bi-cycles and bent eavestroughs, a new car and a camper-in-waiting, hockey nets to the side. He sees the scurry of men and women, restless with time on their hands. Their foxes sit by the curb to lick and preen and wait. A gang of souls sweep through back yards like silent hawks that glide with ill-intent; on patrol, malevolent, at low-loft over fences. Billy cannot believe what he sees. Theirs is to steal and not to forage; so un-like Slim Picker with his truck and his trailer and his purpose. As we are taken from, so we must take back: An act of theft evens the abacus on thin wires of resentment and lives lived hoarding. Birdfeeder after birdfeeder disappears; homemade ones, store-bought ones, squirrel proof cylinders and square suet-dangles gone, gone and other gone. The thing we don't need robs the other thing we don't need, and so on. Billy never considers the sparrows. He never considers the toil and spin of lilies. Nobody does in that neighbourhood.

"They do not retire well, do they?" Billy says to Tulip.

"How do you think their foxes feel?" Tulip replies.

"I don't know why I saved so much junk," Billy wonders.

"It is useless to hoard," says the fox.

VII

Billy rests his eyes on a lone sculpture which stands like an after-thought in a square on the south hill. He reckons it is the concession of a developer's reluctant gift to the people. It perches in front of a backdrop of emaciated parking spaces too thin to prevent dents on car doors. Still, the sculpture is a permanent thing and permanence begets meaning. Billy admires the concession to civic pride but wonders where the extra money comes from. Behold the bronze: Head-bowed in humility, a weld holds a sage-looking man's arse to his bench. Not a single inspired Citizen sits beside him or draws current from his muse. He is utterly alone. Geese-turd coats his head, his shoulders and the iron slats beside him. It is a statue of a writer who props a pad and pencil over crossed legs. Perhaps he composes, or perhaps he prepares useless lottery numbers before he rises and walks towards the variety store over his shoulder. Behind the old turd-besotted artist, a starburst of thin iron bars gets loft, curves and then shimmies over his head, in the wind. The effect gives the flock of Canada geese at the tips an iron majesty, as they organize into an instinctual V-formation.

Once noble, nationally so, Billy regards the ganders as the vermin of Blight; so many, they are everywhere or at least their green cylindrical turds are. Like McCloskey's *Make way for Ducklings* gone-mad, Billy sees geese nest in box-store parking lots; or in reeds by the industrial wastelands where housing stops abruptly and cowers under the bully of row upon row of transport trucks or stack upon stack of rectangular orange shipping containers. The shipping containers are an easy use of land; towering Babels, always at the outskirts where the region to the south meets the Billage to the north and by mutual agreement or squatter's right, deposits all its garbage at the edges. A real-live gander slakes its thirst by a mud puddle next to a series of car dealerships. Billy watches it forage and peck at a plastic sack of wild birdfeed tenderly left by a Samaritan. Between the bullreeds and the grass seed, the bag ferments in the heat of the day. Still, Billy admires the pecking order of good intention, regardless of mildew. He sees the compassion behind it. Tenderness is a lovesome thing.

There is a ding-ding-dinging sound, and a freight train rumbles through the Billage at a classic thirty-degree angle. Fantastic, bulbous script, a full palate of dreamy colour mocks the side of every box car. Billy Hornpipe admires the quizzical font. He wonders about the codifications of affiliation; scribbles of contempt in artistic flash-by and the devil-may-care unification of gangs. For a second, Billy gets the idea that it would be meaningful to be in a gang; that maybe he could be the graffiti artist; but the thrum of clickety-clack rhythm distracts him. A new chorus of sound replaces his trance. It comes from the north: A blat of trumpet, an elephantine pitch of euphonium, the throb of drum and the sweet cry of clarinet. Billy raises his arms. He breathes in, purses his lips and responds to the intrinsic call within his whine-y shawm.

The strong light grows spongy at his feet. Billy realizes it is a sign to return to the centre of the Billage. He shifts to face the waning crescent of his Blue Moon. He glides north past the sculpture with new resolve but then stops. Tulip does not follow.

"You are not coming, are you," Billy says to the fox.

"No, I am not," Tulip replies.

"I can do this, can't I?" Billy asks.

"Yes."

"I have an idea!" Billy cries.

"An idea is a lovesome thing," the fox laughs.

"It is a pleasure to meet you," Billy whispers.

"Same," says the fox. "After all, I saw you standing a-lone … with-out-a-life-of-your-geezis-own."

VIII

Billy Hornpipe's body courses with new energy in his micro-moon: A joy of resuscitation, as if he sits up to take nourishment. There is the taste of fruit cocktail on his lips but the syrup is too sweet, he hates green-grapes and the coffee smells like plastic. He glides down the steep south hill into the centre of town. As lemon juice is to invisible ink, a new graffiti adorns a patterned concrete wall that prevents the banks of the hill from foreclosing onto the side-walk. The wall is a perfect canvas-an inspiration for aerosol. Billy perceives how a letter grows into a word and a word grows into a phrase. The bulbous script appears and disappears like finger wags tucked into memory: *Work Sucks! Sleep in/Let Go! Stub Out Brother-Smoking will KILL YA. Take your Pills! Home is where the TV is…. Don't drink too much…. Retirementos Rule, Boredom Drools. A Shawn is a lovesome thing! Watch your waistline. Don't be reckless! Kiss 4 peace: "Kilroy was here,"* and all that lovey-dovey malarkey.

Lord Bogroll parks his golf cart at the crossroads. Billy sees him cross at the light. He heads toward the coffee shop. Slim Picker pulls his truck into the lot. Straw sets down her wood at the base of a burn barrel, wipes her brow and makes for the entrance. Yeti sips his second cup within. A trumpet blats atop a passing wind.

A fanfare of daylight announces the grandeur of morning. Moon-ray fades and Billy Hornpipe falls from the sky softly, like a quarter in the water or like an oak leaf, back and forth, gusted up, swished down by currents, to land with purposeful resolve on a sidewalk in front of the Obsessa. Billy sees his reflection shine back in the glass of her large window. Background, midground, foreground; past, present and future; he beholds the renovations and dust in the interior, the expression of immediate wonder upon his face and the stalwart coffee shop, behind him. Shawm in hand, meaning-in-mind, he turns to cross the street.

"What are you going to do today, Billy?" Mrs. Hornpipe calls out.

"I don't know," Billy replies over his shoulder.

"You don't have to know," says his wife.

"I know," Billy smiles.

Hunter's Moon

(In which Billy discovers a purpose)

I

Billy makes a stop first before he crosses the road to the coffee shop. He reappears at the recurring place. He walks again along the river road which traces the base of a hill on his right and separates the silver ribbon of river on his left. He misses his fox. Billy basks in the soft orange glow of the Hunter's Moon. He yearns to hunt; to find game, to share and be fulfilled. He admires the magic of twilight, this residual reflection of sun in the night before the big, bright yawn of morning. He rounds a bend, senses movement in the darkness and startles at the sight of a rack of antlers. A buck stops there, in front of him, in the middle of the road. Billy grows quiet. He knows from experience, where there is one deer, there may be more. He gazes at the roadsides but cannot distinguish the shadows. The deer ignores him at first and then arches his neck to sniff. The funky mould of fallen oak leaves mixed with apple cider scents the dew-chilled atmosphere. The hairs on the back of Billy's neck stiffen when the deer turns regally, to regard him. The creature twitches his ears and senses the moment of primordial truth. If the buck charges, Billy knows he is done for. He spies a mastodon bone at his feet and supresses the urge to crush the creature's skull in. Billy Hornpipe sees no need to crush: he has a pension. Mrs. Hornpipe works, the calf is fatted and enough water fills Billy's well. Billy needs a different kind of hunt. Complete communion fills the space between the deer's eyes and Billy's: Their feeling is not unpleasant. The deer senses no danger, lowers his head and exits right. Billy hears cricket-clicks of pronged-hooves on asphalt. As if on a trail of mist, the beast effortlessly scales the hill and disappears into the cedars. There is a vortex and in the vortex, Billy feels the thrum of his heart pulse in his ears. He raises his arms, takes a deep breath, purses his lips and blows on his shawm. There is something beautifully autumn about the sound, a whine of nature which pleases the Hunter's Moon. In the distance, like call and response, he hears the beat of drum, hyena-peels of notes laughing through a clarinet, the blat of trumpet and this time? No snort of euphonium, only the sonorous blare of a valve trombone. Billy spins on his heels and walks toward the cone of lamp-light at the T-junction where the long road leads to the main drag of the Billage. An orange light caresses his neck. Gravity turns him and soon the strobe-effect of this phase of the moon signals his dervish. He whirls and whirls and when the trance lights stop swirling, he stands dutifully in line at the coffee shop: (CC: Ho hum here).

Billy Hornpipe takes an inventory of souls.

He sees the place is packed, so he stands at parade rest, eight citizens back from the counter. Billy hates his ears. He forgets his hearing aids all the time now, sometimes on purpose. Mrs. Hornpipe says he is a man who cuts off his nose to spite his face. Billy accommodates his impairment with closed captions in real-time. He spots the musical instruments first and then shifts his gaze: (Shawm playing). Yeti chats quietly with Lord Bogroll: (Wind passing). A trumpet leans against a clarinet on a spare seat. Straw sits on her own, deep in thought: (Spoon tinkles against mug, here). She silently tests the keys on her euphonium. She appears off stage, like an orphan who auditions a different reality; wonderfully immune from the hub bub and clamour inside. Slim Picker rests an arm on his drum: (Foot tapping). He gazes into twilight and looks out the window at the comings and goings of souls on the main drag. (Man coughing). There are other instruments in the coffee shop. (Cell phones jangling). A melody of people on their own trips, head-bowed, nose-down, fills the shop with twitter and tweet, confluence and current, Wi-Fi and Facebook, fingertip and velocity, misspelled text and a speed, speed, speed that punctuates a distance in the odd seduction of a virtual community: (Retire-mentos yawning).

"Hearing is overrated," Billy says to himself. No wonder Straw sits alone. No wonder Slim Picker toe-taps to his beat. No wonder the Yeti laughs while Lord Bogroll nods his head, conspiratorially.

The line shifts at the approximate pace of a snail smoking weed. Like a mule's haunch, a shiver of frustration ripples, front to back and back to front. Everyone checks the time on their smartphones. ("This is the slowest geezis coffee-joint in the Billage"), a Citizen complains to the woman in front of her. ("It's a franchise you know,") whispers the woman over her shoulder. ("Quantity, not quality" peeps the wren at the feeder). Billy watches the women roll their eyes, all hail-lassie-well-met in the daring intimacy that small talk affords between strangers in quiet public feeding spaces. The exchange amuses Billy and his eyes travel to the front of the line. By chance he notices ol' Ming-the-Merciless, his neighbour from the north-hill. His name is their in-joke; a badge that forges friendship between last-minute chores at the end of the driveway, on Sunday nights. Ming retires well. His waistline becomes him. Billy concedes the point with a pat of vain competition. Judging by the donut bellies around him, at least he is not in last place. Billy thinks Ming-the-Merciless is funny as all get-out. The man makes a quirky small-study out of binge-watching Flash Gordon re-runs in black and white. Billy likes Flash Gordon too and his Merciless interplanetary nemesis, Ming. He admires the villain's sinister leer; the cheesy shape of his ray-gun and the futuristic sil-ver rocket that adorns the movie poster in his neighbour's garage. Ming-the-Merciless: next door neighbour version: is carefree and social: He lends his pruning pole willingly. His beer fridge snug-gles up tight but generous beside the work bench at the back of his man-cave: a fortunate fellow who never skips a beat the second he retires; like he is made for it. He, who works for decades, blinks his eyes and Presto! Home free and the ease of his freedom is beyond natural. Worthy of study, Billy notes.

"I am not a hand-wringer, am I?" he asks Mrs. Hornpipe.

"Put your hearing aids in, Fussbudget," Mrs. Hornpipe answers.

A friend, yes, but upside or downside, Ming refuses to play an instrument. Billy likes him regardless, the way a neighbour just accepts what is and what is not about the world, next door.

The coffee line sets now, in the cement of impatience: (CC: Atomic clock ticking). A citizen weeps and gnashes his teeth: Soon, they all do. Billy gets his *inner grin.* He knows Ming-the-Merciless is a good sport.

"Hey." Billy calls out aggressively to the front of the line.

The murmur in the coffee shop goes to mute. Everyone turns to the cashier in a vain attempt to make Billy disappear.

"You at the head of the line!" Billy continues. "This is a geezis coffee joint: What are you trying to do? Order a steak?"

Fear scratches the air like static. Like a snow-globe shaken violently for effect, Ming-the-Merciless turns to see who the asshole is. He arches his sinister eyebrows and leers with menace. The crowd turns white, gasps-as-one and drifts back and to the sides, like snow. A single soul departs for the exit. The villain observes his rival and picks up the gauntlet.

"Billy, My Man!" The Merciless one laughs. "Set an example: wait your turn or die before us all and miserably so!"

Tension releases: the room explodes with grins of relief, guffaws, knee-slaps and claps on the back. Everyone looks at Billy. There is a genuine envy of friendship in their eyes. Affection grounds the room in a warm hum of peace. The line shuffles forward. The soul who left the building, gazes through the window, makes a pissed off gesture and leaves in a huff. Ming-the-Merciless smiles when he passes by.

"Bring my pruning pole back or I'll Zap you."

Billy Hornpipe makes an effort to reply but is distracted when he hears his name called. He turns.

"Come. Sit with us," Yeti gestures and points to an empty chair.

II

Second Micro Moon

Gravity takes hold. Billy Hornpipe flutters again like a quarter, destined, but in no rush to rest on the sea-bed. The full Hunter's Moon recedes. She grows tiny, so distant in the black expanse and she twinkles like a pinprick.

A wave of anxiety overwhelms Billy and he shivers. He stops sinking and yet again, finds himself in a recurrent place. Cafeteria odours of stew, of burnt coffee and ammonia sting his nostrils— the way sound transmits and traverses' distance. Somewhere a telephone jingles and disrupts the hum of white noise. Billy rocks his head from side to side. He feels a cool dampness of spittle when his cheek presses the pillow.

A metallic clatter of pronged hooves startles him. The buck returns to view. It is skittery and disoriented on a web of suburban asphalt streets. It sniffs a red fire hydrant, steps forward, leaps a small tidy fence and nervously shnibbles the leaves of a mulberry tree. Startled, the creature cringes, then twists and bounds back to the road, faster now. A neighbour bursts outside with his smartphone to document the spectacle. The man presses 'send' and eagerly claims witness to any and all bragging rights. The urban ice breaks and neighbours chat together, full-eyed and full-throated with excitement: ("This feels like T.V.!" A tiny glee-filled boy screams with delight).

The deer runs faster now, stops now and shivers; suddenly leaps now, so wide-eyed and frantic. Billy appears beside the creature. He shares complete communion. Billy gestures; and as if it were never lost, the buck leaps into the safety of a path in the cedars.

Billy rocks his head from side to side and gives protective chase. Neighbour-chatter recedes and Billy stumbles through the cedars onto the campus of a massive university. Billy recognizes the buildings in the pit of his stomach. He starts to sweat.

A large rotunda sits on the throne of a hill. The hill overlooks an expanse into a valley below. Somewhere in the shimmer of light, a vineyard bustles with activity. There are Lebanon Cedars at parade rest along the borders of fields. Billy recognizes background and midground in the vista, but not foreground. In the foreground, a single oak tree ascends skyward. Billy beholds the majestic tower of fertility. The super tree bursts forth like a green fountain over the land. It dwarfs the willows and cottonwood by the silver ribbon of river. Her massive trunk, so wrinkled with life, extends in a starburst of thick limbs, myriad branches, sprays of new growth and clusters of leaves that appear like claps of laughter; clasps of supplication—homages to the fullness of each day from arboreal heights on high. Billy Hornpipe sees the future. For a split-second, the gift of Mrs. Hornpipe's negativity cleanser works and he laughs at a memory.

His gaze ascends the hillside throne to the rotunda. Like trains of ants or bees or like, whatever, students pour into and out of the massive building. Billy is in their midst now. Like the prow of a ship, he sails in a different direction, as if far out to sea. He makes for the white dormitory in the distance to put his feet up and rest in a sanctuary of stillness. The students all gee-gaw and young, loin-filled and vibrant, part like sea foam. Billy sees a young Mrs. Hornpipe, to the right, engulfed in the misty giddy of chatter. Gravity takes him. He changes direction and releases himself into a current of possibilities. It is not unpleasant. He overtakes the students and first-at-the-door, Billy sweeps it open for the young Mrs. Hornpipe. She smiles. Billy smiles and feels the sweet sparks between strangers. He overhears her companion say: 'Well if they are all like this, we'll be fine. I wouldn't kick him out of bed!' Billy, frankly, ignores the woman. Suddenly, he feels a lightness of stomach and a horrifying threat of nausea. Frantically, he searches for a washroom but there are only rooms: Rooms and rooms with numbers on them. A woman, who Billy thinks must be a professor, sighs, grins and walks resolutely through a door. She strides over the threshold of her competence—Let the year begin—and where there is competence, there is purpose and where there is purpose, again perhaps, there is a chance for meaning.

Billy chooses to take four courses. He has no idea what he studies. He marvels at the randomness. He is smarter than he looks and gets very good at something if he sets his mind to it. "If you don't know what you want to do, do something," says the deer. The creature conceals himself in the cedars, safe now, and makes-ready to roam. The deer reminds Billy vaguely of his father and as if, by coincidence, he stifles the urge to throw up. ("Buck up, Billy" is the old joke.)

Billy knows where three classes are but for the life of him cannot find his fourth class. The rooms, rooms, rooms are numbered in sequence. Billy methodically paces off each one. He rounds the bend of the circle within the rotunda, and then falls abruptly into a Black Hole of nothingness: A calculus of unreasonable letters replace numbers and vertigo sets in. Billy consults his timetable. A bell rings from the pit of his stomach, up through his lungs, across the bile of his throat, into the throb in his forehead.

Billy solves things for himself. He asks-not for guidance. Silence reigns supreme. Anxiety is a loathsome thing until it departs.

A voice calls out when Billy stumbles into a cafeteria. Music plays through a speaker. Billy cocks his head. He picks out valve trombone, bass drum, trumpet, euphonium at intervals and clarinet. He plays a few whine-y notes on his shawm. There is complete communion and suddenly, Billy sits with people. A deer bounds past the window outside and silently disappears into the cedars. Billy beholds the group inside. A man in a white lab coat does Sudokus. A woman in mauve scrubs writes. Another soul lays out her collection of crucifixes on the smooth table. A security guard reads the paper, front to back. Billy scans the busy space. The table across from him plays bridge. Another group discusses the merits of free jazz. Foreground, midground, background: At the far end of the room, a woman classifies mushrooms, makes spore prints and slices specimens with a scalpel.

"Why do you not go to class?" Billy Hornpipe asks, exasperated.

"Been there, done that," the voices reply.

"What are you doing here?" Billy cries

"We are stumblebum studying," a woman whispers, one table over.

"Stumblebum what?"

"Doing what we love."

"Are you not afraid to fail?" Billy asks.

"We have pensions," the woman replies.

Sweat returns to Billy's brow. The room begins to rotate, slowly at first and with increasing speed. The pressure against his face feels like a kiss. Billy ascends as he spins. All husk winnows off and golden seed remains in the basin of his heart. A pinprick races towards him. The micro-moon expands, widens, brightens and before he is ready, Billy Hornpipe feels the damp pillow, cool against his cheeks. A new dream replaces an old one like a pea in a shell game. Magically, Billy stumbles out of his old career the way he stumbles into his new one: (CC: Man scratches head, here).

III

Meanwhile back at the coffee shop, Billy hears Yeti's voice. As if in a cheap western he drawls:

"How long you bin playin' shawm, Billy?"

"Not long," Billy replies dutifully and takes a seat.

Billy's 'tryin' to order a steak' wisecrack draws the musicians together. A chair scrapes backward and Straw joins Billy, Lord Bogroll and The Yeti at the table. Slim Picker comes out of his twilight reverie and sits.

"Everyone knows each other?" Billy asks.

"More or less," Slim replies.

"I am just getting to know myself," Billy shrugs.

"We all are," Yeti says. "There is no rush."

A rack of crullers comes out of the oven. Their honey-sweet aroma seduces. Curiously, the group at the table all drink the same thing: Black coffee. Billy notes that each of them refuses to say "*double-double,*" "*triple-triple,*" "*deca-deca*" or "*regular*". Each soul refuses to be inducted into the codifications of urban stupid-speak. It is odd the way their communion completes itself. Yeti tests the waters and says out of the blue: "tik-tok" and then "snap chat". Lord Bogroll guffaws and says "ersatz".

"This coffee smells like a hospital cafeteria," Billy says to break the trance.

"I have skin cancer," Slim Picker replies.

"I had a stent put in," another retiree, a table over, offers.

"Arthritis is not a lovesome thing," Straw laughs.

"What's a little diabetes between friends?" Yeti counters.

"I water the plants of the Billage of Blight," Lord Bogroll says proudly.

"You are lucky to drive a golf cart for a living," Billy adds.

"It has nothing to do with luck," Lord B says gently. "I do it because I want to."

"I want to do something," Billy says out loud.

"So do something then," his table-mates reply in unison. "You're still a spring chicken."

"I am all dressed-down, with nowhere to go," Billy protests.

"The problem, Slim Pickens begins, "is that you have to dump out of this notion of the vineyard."

"What vineyard?" Billy asks sheepishly.

"Silver ribbon of a riber? View from the side of the mountain? Lebanon Cedars standing at parade rest? Background, midground, foreground? Sound familiar?"

"Perfect description of a graveyard if you ask me," Lord Bogroll adds.

"A pretty graveyard though: Give the man some," Straw says in Billy's defense.

"Are you mocking me?" Billy quietly asks.

"Yes," replies the Divine chorus.

"I dream of Straw Island," Straw confesses. "From the air it looks like a treasure map, with coves and groves and super trees where X marks the spot. In the centre, there is an amphitheatre and every day a band of musicians plays jazz to an audience of one. I hated Ornette Coleman but now I love him, and all that free sound he's got goin'. And in the evenings, I find myself on sandy beaches, alone with my burn barrel and all the driftwood I can carry. I burn shit; therefore, I am and my smoke is like a prayer over the land."

"Do you have PTSD?" Billy asks.

"If you mean: 'Am I tired?' Yes, I am, Billy. But I am not done work yet, like Yeti, or Lord B or Slim or you, for that matter.

"Wull, wull, wull, I commuted to the university thar and back, five-day a week, for nigh on thirt'-three yars," Yeti drawls.

"It's his applied psychosis," Lord Bogroll explains rationally. "Don't mind him. Sometimes, he pretends he is in a Western. He repeats himself too. It is a fine line that rubs the edge of delirium, silliness and passion."

Yeti ignores his companion. "Wull, I can speak in tongues—twenny nine languages—including pig-Latin, pil-grims."

"Well, Shirley, you must be the son of gawd," Slim Picker drawls.

"Arf-bay," Bogroll says in pig-Latin and then translates.

"You may be a nit Picker, but you're no John Wayne," Yeti guffaws.

"Geezis. What a good use of time," Billy responds in awe. He tries to follow the thread of conversation: "All I did on the commute was daydream."

"Don't sell yourself short," Straw says. "Daydreams are where reality plays dress-up."

A phone twinkles beside the table of new-found friends. An ersatz digital band plays *Hail to the Chief* in exaggerated time. Mayhem ensues. Like guns drawn from their holsters, Billy reaches defensively for his shawm, Yeti to his trumpet, Slim to his drum, Straw to her euphonium and Lord B to his clarinet.

A well-turned-out young man dressed in mail-order casual, whose trim waistline competes with a perfect beard, weighs in from a table near the window. He sets down his smartphone but keeps his hand on its thigh. Digital, wafer-thin and sexy, Billy sees that the phone and the man are in love, or at least, kind-a going steady.

"Get with it, Champ. You are done like dinner. Salmon up a stream. Eggs laid. Duty done. Like your dead mother and fadder before you and every other Lebanon Cedar. Planted in rows. Scripted in stone. Set in cement. Get a job. Stay with same, same-same for ever like corn, corn corn in a field. Get a house. Amortize. Get married. Have some miserable kids. Put money away or build your lucky pensions. You're sitting around in velour and running shoes and you don't even know how to turn the grindstone off. Good god. By thirty I will make a million dollars and live in an apartment and do exactly what I want. Hope you get to Disneyland."

Billy takes the bait. Why the young man talks at Billy like he is the only soul at the table confuses him. Still, the kid makes a good point, for long ago, Billy's father gets his golden alarm clock a year early; after a nicotine-besotted heart attacks his long row hoe-ed. Even Billy himself doubts his vineyard exists some days, not all.

"Are you cynical?" he asks the kid.

"It's about Bit-coin, Baby," the kid replies and then pauses to take a call: (*Hail to the Chief* plays here).

Billy scrapes his chair back and turns to his friends.

"I have an idea," he declares.

Yeti picks up his trumpet, stands and blats out a note. "If it's a good idea, we should assemble at the statue of the artist for inspiration."

"You mean the Cenotaph by the old River Pub?"

"No. The statue of the guy on the bench with the bird kack," Yeti replies.

"He means the bronze on the south hill, off the main drag, in front of the walk-in clinic and the pop-up computer shop with the strobe-light that gives everyone seizures," Billy says. "I think it's supposed to be a statue of a writer."

"Do not be fooled by cheap imitations," Straw laughs

"Let's make like a bakery truck and haul buns," Lord Bogroll yells with enthusiasm.

The air thins in the Billage. Twilight dissolves. Light cheers the shade and the moods of darkness, somehow shift. Billy gazes over his shoulder, up through the window, at the slice of the waning crescent moon on high. Instruments in hand, the group ascends.

IV

It pleases Billy that the statue remains fixed in place; a constant dependable thing in the Billage of Blight. Lord Bogroll knows where the Region keeps a garden hose and he disappears to attach it to a faucet at the back of the walk-in clinic. Yeti lopes into a sub shop and emerges with a stack of brown paper napkins. Lord B opens the tap; Yeti distributes the napkins and Billy takes the lead to remove the bird-lime from the head of the subject. Yeti scrubs the bench clean-as-a-whistle with Straw, while Slim Picker puts the elbow grease to the long slats that support the V-formation of Canada geese. The bench returns to its former functional glory. The spray of geese quivers in the breeze. A real goose waddles up to see what the fuss is about. The creature assumes the decoy position and preens her back and wing-pits.

Billy sits beside the solitary bronze and throws his arm magnanimously around the smooth cast-iron shoulders like bosom buddies.

"Take my picture," he says.

"Suck in your paunch," Mrs. Hornpipe laughs.

Billy ignores her. He admires writers; not the Rimbaud types but the types who have no angst.

"To be honest," Billy explains, "I like happy writers that have families, love long and all that messy stuff, laugh well and somehow inject adventure and passions into living simply and observing acutely."

"You mean they have pensions?" Straw asks.

"Geez, take a cholesterol pill people," Billy replies. "Seriously, I am tired of reading about the debaucheries of vanity and the bosomy siren calls of muse; apparently in the name of art and as an excuse to fill all self with indulgence."

"The bronze-fellow is not writing Billy," Yeti interjects. "He plays ponies at the track and boxes them for the triactor!"

Billy ignores him:

"The geese are dreams and bird bombs are droppings of rejection letters from story-numb publishers who all want stories about angst and sex, sex and angst."

"Maybe he's ordering a Peatzah," Slim counters.

"Or putting his grocery list together," Lord Bogroll offers.

"No, I agree with Billy," Straw says. "Whatever he puts on his pad is a source for inspiration. We should follow his lead. We should listen. Maybe he has an agent."

"Writing is graffiti for the soul," Billy Hornpipe counters.

"Are you all on blood thinners?" Yeti asks.

Billy picks us his shawm. He takes a breath, purses his lips like a prune and blows into the reed. The high pitch whine sounds exotic and enchanting. As if by reflex, Straw picks up her euphonium and blows. Lord Bogroll moistens his reed and soon a zany hyena-laugh bursts forth from the bell of his clarinet. Boom. Ba-Boom. Boom. Ba-Boom … throbs the drum when Slim Picker picks up their beat. Rising to the occasion, Yeti takes a deep breath, raises his arms, finally shuts his mouth and wails a wail-supreme on trumpet. One by one, harmony aligns and for the first time, they play as an ensemble of serenaders.

The moon vanishes, morning arrives, the commuting starts and another company goes out of business in the Billage of Blight.

Billy feels himself falling.

"We are going to need a valve trombonist," Straw cries out after him.

"Meet me at the Obsessa!" Billy hollers as the statue disappears above him.

V

The Third Micromoon

"Are you comfortable Billy? Is there anything I can get you?" Mrs. Hornpipe asks.

The question startles Billy, for he knows not who he is: or where he is, for that matter.

Billy takes a minute to focus. A fever-chill ripples down his neck and over his shoulders.

"I need a shave," he mumbles.

Mrs. Hornpipe replies but Billy flutters downward like a quarter to the sea bed. For a second, he sees contours of sweet smile on a lunar surface but the vortex sucks him lower. He thinks of *The Honeymooners* and Jackie Gleason in black and white.

When he opens his eyes, the moon is a pinprick again.

"I am tired of this," Billy sighs.

He returns to the recurring space. Billy hears the metallic clicks of propeller screws. For a moment he wonders if his tinnitus re-turns. He rotates 360 degrees to locate the source. A little girl appears before him. She looks vaguely familiar and Billy tries to place her in his lived experience. A value trombone, tethered to her waste, floats light-as-a-feather in her wake.

"Don't you remember me?" The little girl asks. "You ran right past my house on the mountain. I tried to give you flowers but you ran too fast and I could not keep up."

"It is a pleasure to see you again," Billy replies tenderly.

"Can we go fishing now?" The little girl asks eagerly.

Billy holds the little girl's hand and stands at the marina with her. He wants to take her deep-sea fishing but it is too expensive. He settles for the Snapper Boat. The Snapper Boat fills in procession, like Noah's ark. Every species of gee-gaw boy and party girl streams in, walks up the gangplank and rushes to the top deck to assemble at the bow. The ticket booth approaches, much too fast for Billy's liking. He removes his wallet from the back pocket of his shorts, lowers his gaze, concentrates and skims out money.

"Wouldn't you rather catch a marlin, Bub?" a voice says.

Billy raises his head. An old nautical man with a kindly face stands beside him. His waistline is taut and his brown skin looks like rope. Turns out the deep-sea boat has a last-minute cancellation.

"There's room for you and the girl. Tackle, bait and gas does not pay for itself but I'll give you a deal," the skipper offers.

Billy gazes down at the little girl.

The little girl looks up at Billy and beams.

"I just want to fish with you," she says.

The propeller screw whirls off into deeper parts of the ocean. Billy feels buoyant. He fills his lungs, purses his lips like a prune and blows on his shawm.

Slowly, surely, he rises; happy with the knowledge he made sure his children had fun.

Wolf Moon

(In which Billy finds meaning and forms a band of serenaders)

I

Billy surfaces again along the river-road which traces the base of the hill on his left and separates the silver ribbon of river on his right. He smells the pungent oily smells of cedars and feels brightness on the back of his neck. Absentmindedly, he rubs and then dries the sweat on the thigh of his track pants. Billy bathes himself in a limelight that illuminates the asphalt stage up to where the T-junction points left, down the long road, to the main drag of the Billage. Limelight mixes with lamplight like a rehearsal at the crack of dawn.

Billy hears a howling in the darkness behind him. A lamentation replaces the sweet whine of shawm in his ears. The howling puzzles Billy. Sprinklings of black thirty-second notes pepper the air, in front of him. A night-breeze composes a harmony of mood that shifts in intentional rhythms like breath. Yes, lamentations; but Billy also parses urgencies, yearnings, strivings and passions in the sound. Curiously, he thinks of end, cause and effects, where meaning, action and results grow to take on a composition of their own or at least, a momentum of melody. Billy knows what comes next. Impatiently, he glides forward until the gravity of the moon creates her solar resistance. Slowly he turns. He feels the vortex. In the increasing velocity he observes the strobe-pulses of the phases of the moon in his temples. An aroma of wood smoke fills Billy's nostrils. He hears the blat of trumpet. A Gershwinian giggle of clarinet makes him laugh and resolves all tension on the chord.

His Dervish complete, Billy sets himself down lightly on the little stone patio, between the abandoned restaurant on the left and the Obsessa to the right, along the main drag of Blight across from the coffee shop.

Straw gets leverage with a crow bar and pries off a board.

"What kept you Billy," Yeti asks.

"I went fishing," Billy replies.

"Billy you should see this!" Slim Picker cocks his thumb and points:

NOTICE OF PUBLIC MEETING

PROPOSED ZONING BY-LAW AMENDMENT

A public meeting will be held to consider an application

for a wet market.

Your input and insight will inform and shape plans that meet the

needs of our community.

Meeting Dates:

Garbage Day (Monday) and Ad Match Day (Tuesday)

Time: Before sunrise.

"This could be our big break, Billy!" Slim says urgently.

"We could re-purpose the space," Yeti muses.

Straw stands to stretch her back and roll her shoulders. "I could sell my burn barrels here and Slim could sell all the junk he finds at the curb like a rag-and-bone man."

"Absolutely!" Slim nods. "And Lord Bogroll could hang all his flowers and sell cuttings and seeds!"

"We'd have a source of water. There is a faucet around the corner at the back of the Obsessa," Lord Bogroll offers. "We'll need to wash down the patio every day Billy, if you intend to sell fresh Canada geese. Hygiene is important, you know. You said they are everywhere. We can re-purpose the vermin and put them to good use. Nobody sells fresh goose-burgers in Blight! We'll corner the market!"

"… and thereby: have a hand in shaping plans to meet the needs of our community," Yeti laughs: (CC: trumpet fart here).

The passion of his friends to do something meaningful, to be useful, tempts Billy sorely. He forgets, for a moment, his grand idea for greater involvement. It is unbecoming when greed trumps contribution. Billy hesitates in the space between his senior's moments. He wonders whether to lead or to follow.

A tall man wears a yellow shirt with green Billage of Blight lettering on his chest. He gazes into the broad window of the Obsessa, presses down a lick of errant hair, hears the kerfuffle beside him and strides over to the group. He notes they all wear track pants and running shoes. Straw sets her crowbar down and pushes it under a shrub with her foot.

Billy approaches the tall man and reads the script on his shirt.

"I see you are with the Billage," Billy remarks. "What is your role here?"

"I am the Mayor of Blight," the mayor says. "Are you the Billage idiot?"

"He doesn't get out much," Yeti says on the beat of Billy's defense.

"Listen to me, you Retirementos. The Canada goose is our symbolic Bird of Canada. She is part of the sacred circle. Like your Billage Council, the avian stands for cooperation and a geezis communication-of knowing when to lead and when to follow. Besides, the Obsessa has first dibs on the patio. She wants to sell cannabis here. It's brilliant really, for it not only serves the bottom line and fine-food interests of Obsessa patrons, whenever-the-hell-it-is she opens; it increases sales with the munchie-crowd up and down the main drag. Our sub, pizza and variety stores will flourish. It's about revitalization, baby … and tattoos."

"Are you on blood thinners? The notice says 'wet market' not cannabis shop," Slim points out, with some resolve, to the mayor.

"Attention grabber, figure of speech. It will all go viral and we need a good turnout."

"Will you at least rent us the industrial strength espresso machine inside the Obsessa?" Billy asks. "It's not doing anything. It has no purpose. It sits vacant until whenever the renovations get done and the place re-opens."

"Why would I do that?"

"Because we … We ARE … the Stumblebum Waytes, a band of strolling musicians whose sole purpose is to serenade the Billage for small gratuities," Billy announces triumphantly.

Yeti, Lord Bogroll, Straw and Slim Picker's collective mouths drop open.

"You mean play for money?" the mayor asks.

"No, for espresso," Billy clarifies.

"We will beautify Blight and celebrate important things. We will fulfill our civic duty," Billy continues. We will make a gaw-damn contribution and be useful."

"Till death do us part," Lord Bogroll adds with maybe a bit too much geezis gravity.

The mayor steps back and howls.

"Why this is too-much-of-a-muchness! It is not something, I can decide on my own, in twilight, under the gaze of a Wolf Moon! Come to the Town Hall meeting on Garbage Day. Arrive early. Audition for us and then we will give you an answer. Do not expect miracles. Good day!"

The Yeti raises his trumpet and passes wind.

"We are going to need someone to play valve trombone, Billy," Straw says sensibly. "All for one," Billy replies decisively. "My God, I'm back!" (CC: crowd cheers, here).

II

Billy walks up to the wide window of the Obsessa and looks past his reflection. He sees the coffee shop behind him and gazes into the interior of the restaurant. Hospitable like a hospital, he smirks. A white sheet drapes along the full length of the bar. A drop cloth covers two tables. Ambient light yaws open dark recesses and anterooms. For some unknown reason, a most beautiful specimen of geode sits on a flat surface like a heart open to crystalline joy. Billy sees dust particles float in air. The metallic ring of skill-saw startles him. Only then, he notices the worker-bees, two men and a woman. *Sensibly*, the woman wears a mask but the men are testosterone-stupid. One of them stamps out a cigarette on the floor.

He kicks the butt over by a sheet of drywall. Billy knows he could murder a cigarette but fights the urge. The logo, *Havisham's Reno's*, adorns the back of the worker's overalls. The white mist creates a cadaver-effect that transforms the workers into strange caricatures of human beings in a geezis Charles Dickens story. Billy watches them lurch between tasks. Motion slows and he observes them thoughtfully, like buoyant fish silently feeding-with-intent, in an aquarium. The woman darts off and returns with a pail of Polyfilla. She globs it on, patches a long seam and uses her trowel smoothly in deft strokes, like an artist, or like a surgeon. Billy realizes the Obsessa will open whenever hell freezes over. Maybe it is a tax write-off in the Billage of Blight. He shifts his gaze to the corner of the renovated space. There stands the object of his lust: the industrial strength espresso machine. A parted drop cloth, like a gown that will not be tied at the crack, reveals her sensuous form and majestic design. She basks in the warm glow, like a copper Grecian goddess: demure, modest, confident—sexy, frankly in a machine kind-of-a-way. Billy thinks of all the weddings he attends with Mrs. Hornpipe; how gravity pulls men in congregation to the bar; how thick coffee begets brandy begets biscotti—the long wait to feasts at Christmas and reunions of memory with friends.

Besides all that, Billy notes the obvious resemblance between the espresso machine and Flash Gordon's rocket ship. How could he not? She adorns herself aerodynamically with rounded bullet crown, levers and valves that twist soundlessly with calibrated precision. She purrs and hisses; lights red and steams before lift-off. Billy loses himself in his window-reflected reverie.

A image appears beside him and cheerfully reads his thoughts:

"We can haul it up in my truck to the statue of the writer," Slim Picker offers.

"Perfect place to rehearse," Billy replies.

Billy loves to gaze into the window of the Obsessa. Like an oracle, the glass tells him everything and it tells him nothing. Billy gets silly. Foreground, midground, background, he laughs.

Billy is not only privy to his soul, but to his mind and then to his body and beyond that into his surroundings. Who gets to do that, he wonders? As if under water, before his very eyes, in vivo, some might say, *Havisham Reno's* continues its eternal restoration. A skeleton takes form; only Billy says it like Billage: A Skellington takes form; flesh grows over the hard bones of structure and suggests the promise of new life, ambient space, new menu, New Management, Coming Soon and any other construction of hope. Billy says to himself, he better get a resume in. Maybe he could be a barista. Involuntarily, a thought twinkles behind his eyes.

In the intimacy of affection, the glass of the window kisses Billy's forehead, his cheeks, his chin and his lips. Billy sees himself, the way Mrs. Hornpipe might; innocently, free from doubts with only yearnings to know, to know perhaps deeper; to know a deeper truth; to understand everything, to mend him and be tender. Billy pauses and breathes. A pain attacks his heart. He feels the present but the present makes him sheepish. Mrs. Hornpipe guards him against the howl of wolves. She drives off his vanities, all hand-wringings and angsts so much so that Billy stays silly and blinks again.

The glass of the Obsessa mutates into carnival glass. In the light of the Wolf Moon, Billy sees his buffoonery. He sees clown stripes on baggy velour sweat pants. Oily black grease darkens his chin like a five-day beard. White pancake makeup, enhances the frown upon his garish red lips: My God he looks like a Stumblebum, a Vagabondo, a Tramp!

Yes, he looks feral; but Billy knows that laughter, once in a while, is a gift of humility. The carnival glass creates an odd effect: His head swells and his waistline shrinks when he plays with the angle of moonlight.

Closed caption appears on the window: (Birds Chirping). (Insect's chittering). (Cars commuting). (Cell phones ringing). (Musicians playing). Billy finds it odd to see reflections of his future behind him. He wonders if his future faces him, too. Vertigo sets in and Billy spins. Thankfully, a cell phone sprinkles *Hail to the Chief*, like pepper into the air. Billy sneezes and turns from the window to face the present.

"What are you trying to do? Order a steak?" a mocking voice says.

Billy sees it is the well-turned-out, mail-order-casual young man with the trim beard, the trim waistline and the smartphone—the Bit-coin Kid from the coffee shop across the road.

"You look more like a penny to me," Billy counters.

"I am going to make a million by the time I am thirty," the Kid says as if by rote.

Billy respects that the young are fabulously wealthy in their own minds. He changes tack:

"You remind me of a young me."

"Hard to appreciate, when you're past your due-date, Pops."

"My head is still in the clouds like yours," Billy says.

"Then why are you wearing velour sweat pants?"

Billy sighs. "It's functional attire," he explains.

"You actually still shop in Blight?" the Kid says incredulously.

"Listen to me. At my age, I can do what I want, when I want, for as long as I want. I am master and commander of my own space. I dominate time, but do not control it. The atomic clock still ticks, but I wind the watch, son."

"Are you going to paint the bathroom today?" Mrs. Hornpipe interjects.

"Honey, I am making a point here," Billy snaps in the unbecoming way of husbands. "May I get a word in edgewise? Is the wolf at our door?"

"Somebody has to wear actual pants," Mrs. Hornpipe replies.

Billy ignores Mrs. Hornpipe. He forgives the mean wisdom of wives.

"Do you know how to play valve trombone, Kid?"

"Is there any money in it?" the well-turned-out, on-the-go young man replies.

"Espresso is a timeless crypto-currency, Bub."

"Yes, I can play valve trombone," the mail-order kid lies. "I played trombone in high school, and trumpet and I was in a quartet and a garage band."

Billy hands him the valve trombone.

"See if you can get a note out of this."

The Bit-coin Kid lifts the instrument, places it on his shoulder, tries the slide, puckers his lips and stretches the beautiful note. A trumpet blats somewhere in response to the call.

"Welcome to Stumblebum Waytes, son. Put your cell-phone on mute. You are in the band and you're going to need a new name," Billy says with relief.

Billy Hornpipe walks the lad proudly over to the patio where the rest of the band still dreams of wet markets and meaning.

Straw stops prying off another board and looks up.

"It's that Bit-coin Kid from the coffee shop. What's your two cents worth today, son?"

"A penny saved is a penny earned?" Yeti laughs.

"In for a pound, in for a penny," Slim warns.

"Penny for your thoughts, whippersnapper," Lord Bogroll challenges.

The kid turns out to be a good sport. He raises his valve trombone and plays with urgency, courage and conviction.

Youth is a lovesome thing, Billy notes.

"Monday is Garbage Day, Two-Bits. Show up when the moon is full. Tomorrow, Stumblebum Waytes auditions for the mayor. It's an important gig."

"Does the Billage have a line on Bit-coin?" Two Bits asks.

The light changes, a wolf howls and Billy looks into the eyes of the band. The band accepts the Kid in complete communion.

III

Billy awakes in a rush. He forgets his hair brush and his hair looks like wolf's bane.

"Silver becomes you," Mrs. Hornpipe says, in the bedside warmth of side-by-side bodies before dawn.

Billy rocks his head on his pillow and laughs. He picks up his knees and folds his hand across his chest. He mocks death's repose. Current flows from within. Besides, through their bedroom curtain, Billy comforts himself in the pale light. He opens his face and gazes fully into the Wolf Moon. Billy stretches the soles of his feet, his insteps and fights an onset of ache.

"I am still not a hundred percent," he mumbles.

Billy picks out words lazily in the grog of sleep and tries to say 'wolf's bane' in a sentence.

"I love you, Billy Hornpipe," Mrs. Hornpipe says and then ignores him and rolls over.

"Same," Billy replies simply and wipes sleep-dirt from his eyes.

Billy notes there is no sweat on his pillow and drool no longer seeps from the corners of his lips. Morning inventory complete, he rises. His rocking stumblebum gait helps to replaces his need to whirl like a dervish on the road that separates the cedars on the left from the silver ribbon of river on the right. A thought pushes its way outside in. Billy remembers Tulip, his fox, fondly. Urgency befalls him. The thought kindles in Billy's mind, bursts into flame and Billy knows it is time to do something productive. Modestly, he closes the bathroom door and goes pee-pee.

"Are you doing the laundry today?" Mrs. Hornpipe mutters. "I have to go into work soon."

"Somebody has to wear the pants," Billy says directly to the oracle in their mirror.

Billy appears, as if across a threshold, inside the council chamber of the Billage of Blight. He watches a citizen fold down a well-worn, plush seat and snuggle into the amphitheatre. It pleases Billy to see Stumblebum Waytes on time. The somber political air over-warms the space but the atmosphere feels snug-as-a-bug-in-a-rug. Billy Hornpipe's band of serenaders lingers by a functional and very boring silver coffee urn. Billy giggles at the groggy tableau in front of him. Each soul unfolds their wings the way a turkey vulture hunches high on a dead tree limb, and then turns its back to anticipate morning's warmth from the East. The coffee urn does its civic duty. It plunks and shugs; hisses and gurgles and everyone hopes the red light comes on soon. A half-full cup of dirty brown water stands impatient vigil beside clusters of plastic creamers. Two-Bits impatiently decants another and sets it aside indignantly. What a dope.

He reaches into a bowl of red-stripe mints and plucks one. It is free after all, and there are lots of them. Billy aches for a cup of espresso.

Straw beholds the auditorium. Lord Bogroll admires the after-thoughts of plants. Billy watches him snip a brown leaf with his finger nails. Yeti opens a pack of strawberry jam and spreads it on a stale croissant with a white plastic knife. Slim Picker loads his pockets with cellophane wrapped cookies. The casual theft reminds Billy that it must be Monday. He pulls out his shawm and with a nod, prepares to conduct Stumblebum Waytes. Straw hefts her euphonium. The Yeti fingers his trumpet valves. Slim adjusts the straps on his drum. Lord Bogroll moistens his reed and Two-Bits quietly pumps his slide. Billy sees that Two-Bits' head is already in the metaverse. The Boy dances to the beat of a different dream. A natural rhythm besots his imagination like breathing. He thinks he knows, but he does not know and the other who cares? Billy likes the kid.

A gavel clacks wood and all ears trace the sound downwards to the curved podium at the front. Straw nudges Billy and Billy turns towards the proceeding. Billy hates his hearing aids. Yeti rolls his eyes and massages the muscles of his arm. The uniformity of velour track pants distinguishes them all in the gleamy twilight of Billage proceedings. Straw turns out well, but Billy thinks the boys could have tidied up just a bit more. Billy rubs his chin and is glad he remembers to shave. This is professional; he winks to no one in particular.

Down below, to the left, a door swishes open, silently, the way a hospital door swishes open and closes without a sound. A clerk hands a note to the mayor of the Billage of Blight. Billy sees the medallions draped across his chest like an ephod on the priest of Moses. Bejewelled with civic responsibility, sapphire, ruby and amethyst blink like Urim and Thummim on the unholy breastplate of politics. Billy guffaws and makes no mistaken identity faux pas, this time. Yeti pokes his ribs.

One by one, Billy observes the council women and the council men. A smell of cannabis pervades the air. Billy notes it is not the ancient, sexy outlaw smell. Billy smells the new thing.

He smells wet socks frankly. A man in a black suit stands and turns his back to the audience. He adjusts his chair and Billy sees the words *Havisham Reno's* stitched across his shoulders. It stuns Billy that a man sews his logo on the back of formal clothes. Billy reminds himself he wore a suit for thirty-three years. A woman in sensible navy blue, with *senstible* waistline looks stern. She taps her microphone and the amplified pop makes everyone cringe.

A gavel snaps wood again: Like a long-forgotten millers' wheel on a silver ribbon of riber, the Billage of Blight proceeds, round-and-round in perpetuity. It spills water, wastes water and turns un-hindered—propelled by streams of ennui, the spoor of inefficient ditherings.

"We are here to hear the application to re-purpose the abandoned patio beside the Obsessa," the mayor announces. "But before we proceed, I have invited Stumblebum Waytes to play for you to commemorate the proceedings."

Billy startles at the amplified cue over the microphone. He stands and leads the Waytes to the front.

"Let's do *"Battle of Jericho,"* Billy whispers.

He wets the reed of his shawm and opens his elbows wide. On the beat he lifts his instrument into the air and brings his elbows down-on-demand. A whine of shawm begins. Trumpet joins, followed by the beautiful snort of euphonium. Slim Picker drums the melody-line so dramatically; the audience feels a thrill of shivers. Swept into bop-moments of rhythm, the clerk forgets herself completely. Spontaneously, she rises in place and sings: "Jo-shu-a-fot-the-ba-ddle-of-Jer-i-cho," baritone, like Tennessee Ernie Ford. Her voice descends from on high like an angel. Lord Bogroll comes in next, with hyena-sounding treble notes and Two-Bits empties each lung breathless, off interior moorings, with a crescendo of muted march-steps on slide. Stumblebum Waytes whirls in a circle of moonlight while they play. The motion becomes them.

When the last sixteenth note plinks the air, like a bubble, the chamber grows silent. Billy dries his eyes and nods to Stumblebum Waytes. The band returns the nod: There is complete communion. The room is so quiet, Billy wonders if they even played.

A gavel spanks wood.

A regal voice decrees: "The application for a cannabis shop on the patio is awarded to the Obsessa. There shall be no wet market in Blight. A contract is hereby granted to *Havisham Reno's*. So, spoken: (Gavel spanks again. Crowd murmurs. Chairs squeak). Work to commence immediately!"

Billy removes the reed from his shawm, dries it on the thigh of his track pants and returns it to its case. Slim tightens the skin-keys on his drum and inspects his sticks for wear. The brass section purges its gob on the chamber floor, absentmindedly, the way musicians do, and Lord B breaks his clarinet down into three and snaps the case shut. The band ascends to the back of the amphitheatre and exits softly, through the main door into the twilight of the lobby. Billy notes obligatory Group of Seven paintings in gilt frames, hang along the wall. He sees photographs of ribbon cuttings and proud tattoo shop owners. A council woman of importance, fixed in time like a silent movie, stands smiling beside a non-descript developer with a *'Snidely Whiplash'* mustache. Greed is a loathsome thing, Billy smirks.

Billy Hornpipe turns to face Stumblebum Waytes. He opens the note in his hand, slipped to him by the Clerk on his way out. He clasps it to his chest like a defibulator:

"It's officially, official," Billy sighs. "We passed the audition. The industrial strength espresso machine is ours for a nom-i-nal low-mon-th-ly pay-ment."

"Then play on, Billy! I'll get the truck," Slim Picker laughs and strides off to the parking lot.

IV

Billy loves the solid clunk of a truck door slamming. The peculiar sound of metal differs from the dainty-snick of car doors. Billy knows there is work to do. Slim Picker is already at the back of the truck and lowers the gate on his trailer. The copper espresso machine stands poised to lift off in all her steam and glory. Straw's burn barrel hitches a ride, along with a chainsaw and a red container of gasoline. On this day, Slim gathers up the desires of good intention by the Retiremento-class. The back of his truck fills to the brim with a discard of personal bucket list: a litany of never-used mountain bikes, rowing machines, snowshoes, tennis and squash rackets, guitars and pianos; the afterthoughts and misfires of make-believe wishes. Gratefully, Billy sees Lord Bogroll putter dutifully, at the back of the Walk-in clinic. He attaches a hose, untangles it and drags the unruly coil behind the statue of the writer. He returns to the back, cranks the faucet, narrows the nozzle and soon the silver spray means business. Efficiently, the hard shower removes the bird lime from the shoulders and head of the bronze perfect thing. The shower rinses the iron slats on the bench, next. It sluices away filth, the way pond water rinses dust off a goose's oily back. In the foreground, by the curb, a beaked-thing deposits a green turd and waddles away. A wet, growing stain on the concrete disturbs Billy like a flashback. It reminds him of the way blood defiles white sheets and he shudders. Tenderly, he grabs an orange cloth and dries the recesses of the writer's face. He pats the forehead and daubs the eyes. Carefully, he shifts focus and gently ministers to the ears. A breeze comes up: Billy cringes involuntarily and looks skyward at the quivering metal V-formation. He watches the iron birds get loft overhead, made lighter by a release of imaginary bowels.

"The statue is in torment," Billy declares. "We shall name him/her Prometheus. He/she/it shall be Stumblebum Waytes' muse. We/us/them steal fire from the gods and we protect self/other/us from ancient turkey vultures (they/them/turds) that populate fields in Blight."

"Part and participle, Lord Bogroll laughs. "We'll clean it/it every morning under the moonlight."

"Like a ritual," Billy replies. "Then, we'll get published."

"I keep telling you, Billy. The man is doing Ad-Match," Yeti interrupts. "It is Tuesday in his mind: Tuna is on sale for 99 cents." Yeti blows confidently on his espresso not yet made.

Straw laughs and busies herself at the back of Slim's pick-up truck.

"Help me get the burn barrel off," she asks.

Billy Hornpipe leaps to the occasion, like the go-to guy he was, is and still wishes to be.

"You should not be lifting, Billy," Mrs. Hornpipe says.

"Who dies and makes you a doctor?" Billy replies indignantly.

"Take a pill," Mrs. Hornpipe replies.

Billy bends at the knees and puts his back to it. Together with Straw, he lifts the burn barrel out of the back of Slim's truck. Straw removes her chainsaw and fills it with gas. She spills not a drop. Standing, she inspects her surroundings the way women with intention can.

In the spontaneity of shared motivation, Lord Bogroll fetches a coil of extension cord. He goes to the back of the walk-in clinic, plugs prongs into live current, and carefully unspools the green snake. There are no knots and he connects the cord to the espresso machine. Satisfied, Lord Bogroll fills the industrial urn, tamps the espresso vessels and hits the switch. A red light comes on: Stomachs rumble, noses poise for aroma and they await liftoff. Yeti is happy now.

"You are our high priest of caffeine," says Billy. "I anoint you with affection, Bub."

"Angels and demons," Lord Bogroll replies.

Billy Hornpipe's closed caption returns: (Birds chittering, Wolf howling). He chuckles. Billy loves to say the word, "chitter." He associates it with a tintinnabulation of chimes; like the ways girls giggle in recurring dreams.

"Where is Two-Bits?" somebody says.

A valve trombone slides a defiant *wrop* in the twilight. A long note stair-steps in crescendo and emerges in muted roars. A fanfare for sleepy-eyed youth heralds the moon-light, self-centres it, wobbles it like a vinyl record on a spindle, until the needle takes hold and enough music awakens to finally make sense of noise.

"Here me is!" Two-Bits cries. He gets the pronoun wrong, doesn't care about grammar and busily texts another internet best friend. Somewhere a teacher in the Billage of Blight rolls her eyes. A civic phone lights up and the word-police are on duty.

"A penny for your thoughts, shithead," Slim Picker grumbles and sees he is late for work.

"I am used to working from home, on Zoom," Two-Bits argues, and spreads his arms out from the trim of his waist.

While the espresso machine rumbles, Straw unleashes the chain saw and cuts down a mountain ash tree in front of the walk-in clinic. Emerald ash borer infects all the trees now, in the Billage of Blight. Dutch elm disease takes her run in the seventies, followed by a leprosy that rots beech bark from the core out. Straw knows the arboreal law. She re-purposes bramble for a greater good. She stuffs branches into her burn barrel. She tidies the neighbourhood, like a hair stylist open for business.

"Fire cleanses," Straw explains to no one in particular.

Lord Bogroll seizes the meaningful moment. "I shall replant the land with super trees!" he declares and gestures with his right hand, like a green-thumb prophet.

Bogroll's vision of the emerald beyond triggers Yeti. Master of post-traumatic languages on the perpetual commute, he lapses into a Berlitz hustle of fortune-cookie speak.

"Good things will happen soon."

"A surprise awaits."

"Your waistline shall become you: (Pen scratches on note pad)."

It pleases Billy that the band is happy. Satisfied, he throws his arm around the bronze Prometheus and chats to a captive audience.

"I think we should get a dog, Billy," Mrs. Hornpipe says.

"I had a fox," Billy counters.

"That's different. The routine and the exercise will be good for you."

"You don't have to clean up after a fox," Billy admits.

"Are you kidding?" Mrs. Hornpipes replies.

Two-Bits walks over to the iron bench.

"Why do you fixate on the writer," he asks. "Everything is online."

Billy patiently explains that the writer takes field notes and observes.

"Come on. Nobody reads observations," Two-Bits groans. "Too many words, besides, it's about reaction and angst, Blog and make-believe expertise. Okay to put a little sex in it, too."

Billy ignores the Boy's two cents' worth of bramble. He turns and addresses the statue.

"Look, at his eyes, Two-Bits! It is like he searches the ocean in sight of the thing. Master and commander of his own ship. He scans waves; sees a flick of tail, a fluke; maybe a fan-tail and the massive lines of leviathan, hidden in brine. He scribbles. He laughs. He cries. But for tenacity, each book is a greyte creature that offers herself up. When she looks into a writer's eyes, she looks into his heart. Each voyage, each sighting of the whale is a gift to all of us. We should be thankful, shit-head."

Billy's lecture disgruntles Two-Bits.

"Tik-Tok," he smirks in reply. He stoops, scrolls and then walks away from the boring statue to return an important call.

"Billy, you made the *Billage Bluster!*" Yeti walks over to the bench, folds the spine of the newspaper and shows Billy Hornpipe a picture of Billy and the mayor, next to the coffee urn at the council meeting. Yeti lapses into fortune cookie-speak again. "A choice awaits"

Stumblebum Waytes gathers around the iron bench.

"Why is it just you in the picture, Billy? We were all there," Two-Bits says indignantly.

The photograph puzzles Billy.

"I am not sure," he whispers.

Billy wants to yack more about Prometheus; about rejection letters, bird-lime and publisher whims but an approaching white car interrupts the band. It flashes its headlights and pulls up to the curb. A door snicks shut. Billy recognizes the clerk from the council meeting. Breathless, she hands Slim an official looking letter, cream-coloured on good stock, sealed by the mayor—a ceremonial keepsake on Billage Stationary or something. Slim reads the letter and passes it to Straw. From Straw, the letter goes to Lord Bogroll while Yeti reads over his shoulder. Finally, the official-thing transfers to Two-Bits who brings it closer to and then farther from his eyes.

"What the hell is this? I only read texts," he says.

Two-Bits dutifully hands the letter to Billy.

Billy pauses and remembers his manners. He looks up at the clerk.

"It is a pleasure to see you again. By the way, you nailed *Battle of Jericho*. Brought the house down. We loved your Tennessee Ernie Ford baritone."

"I was actually channelling my inner Rosemary Clooney, but thank you anyway," the clerk says, slightly miffed. "I see from your clothes that you are retired," she sniffs.

Billy smoothes the thighs of his velour track pants, sneaks a peak at his waistline and picks at an errant thread.

"We are that," he says to the Clerk.

"What shall I tell the mayor?" the Clerk asks.

"We'll get back to you," Billy replies. "Thank the mayor for the loan of the espresso machine. Let him know our first payment will be by the light of the next full moon."

The clerk turns. A car door closes elegantly and she disappears into the twilight.

The atmosphere changes. Billy Hornpipe's pulse quickens. He notices an intrusion of dawn in the east; soon the light will be over Serenity Acres.

Yeti breaks the swoon:

"An ill-wind blows west."

"An unpleasant event will occur."

"A choice is at the cross-roads…."

Billy interrupts his imaginary friend.

"Brother, you're speaking fortune cookie again."

Startled, Yeti reverts to the King's English. "Good God," he replies.

Two-Bits prefers plain-speak but opts to remain quiet.

Yeti clutches the letter and points to the contents.

"Billy? What a horror story! Do you see the length of this geezis list? Billage Council has a million ceremonial openings lined up for us to commemorate with music and fanfare: Tattoo shops, teeth whitening emporiums, nail clinics; three more sub-huts, ten more weed joints and another pop-up fireworks store. I'll tell you this for sure: Stumblebum Waytes may dress like rubbie-dubs but we're not turncoats. This feels way too much like work. We are re-tired. Good God. We can write our own ticket, remember? I have a pension, after all."

"We could do it if they pay us in Bit-coin, Billy," Two-Bits whispers.

"Billy?" Straw asks. "Don't you think we are passed the days of doing something for the sake of doing something? Where is the meaning in that? Everything will go out of business in six months anyway. That equals a lot of wood—a lot of stuff to burn. It's not like we're selling out; it's like we're going guerilla."

"I'm not doing a thing on Garbage Day," Slim Picker declares.

"… or Ad-Match Day for that matter…."

"If there's plants, I'll water them Billy," Lord Bogroll whispers loyally.

"Input duly noted," Billy replies. "How close are we to the next round of espresso, Lord B? Is it perked yet?"

Billy wets his reed and fits it into the mouthpiece. He purses his lips like a prune, breathes in and blows. The shawm begins its high pitch whine. A note spills out, then another: whole notes, sixteenth notes, swirls of thirty second notes, sharps and flats, you know, the salt and pepper of the thing…. The melody gathers together like leaves in an eddy and lifts like a dervish into the remaining moonlight.

"Are you ready for a coffee?" Mrs. Hornpipe calls out from the kitchen.

Billy thinks of wind chimes.

"I didn't sleep well," he realizes and then sits up.

V

Start and startle; Billy Hornpipe comes to ground. His eyes snap open and sight returns. A demon rests on his shoulder. Irked to be discovered, Billy's demon flits off. The creature honks, gets loft and joins his squadron-on-high, in V-formation.

"Good riddance!" Billy says, and then rubs the stubble on his chin.

Mrs. Hornpipe slumbers by Billy's side. He turns, throws his arm around her waist, kisses her shoulder, nestles and feels the warmth only a husband gets to feel.

Billy looks directly into the Wolf Moon through the framed oracle of the bedroom window. The Wolf Moon gazes back indifferently. A twilight thought, unbidden, intrudes. "Nobody looks. My life is mine own," Billy says resolutely.

"So do something about it, Billy," Mrs. Hornpipe mumbles.

Reality teaches hard lessons if men possess a courage to listen.

Billy unclasps his pious hands from his chest. He continues lying on his back now, before dawn, and mocks what it feels like to be a corpse in repose. He rises.

"I am ready to live," Billy Hornpipe says to the audience of spirits that inhabit his mind. He hears clusters of hurrahs and hand claps and pockets of cat-calls and hoots. At the podium of his inner being, Billy turns to the right, raises his arms and hears joy. He turns to the left, raises his arms to conduct but hears mutter and mumble. An atomic clock ticks like a metronome. Billy Hornpipe's newly minted power amuses. He repeats his turn to the right and repeats his turn to the left, whirls like a dervish and blends the whole mess together into the everyday vortex called living: (Birds chittering. Wolf howling).

Mrs. Hornpipe slumbers. Her sweet breath keeps time with her heart beat. Billy marvels at gifts of peace bestowed like puffs of night-breeze on a quiet porch.

He looks on high and grows impatient with the neutrality of the third quarter phase of moon. The center axis divides half the moon in white on the left and half the moon in black on the right like some sort of cosmic 50–50. In the bathroom, Billy tidies up. He skips the oracle in his reflection. He skips the cedars, the silver ribbon-of-riber on his right; the long road to the main drag and finds himself pulled in by swirling aromas and rising smoke with the scents of mountain ash and espresso in his nostrils.

Dew besotted, in the chill-moisture of twilight, Billy sits beside Prometheus. He loves the installation art—its hard permanence, its reliability. Like the statue, Billy observes things slightly-out-of-view. He begins to accept the gift of grace in the space between events. He no longer rushes while others watch. Billy stretches his legs and feels his back press firmly against iron slats. He returns old sighs to their oblivion of origin. He watches now, while other's rush.

A good blaze already burns, in the barrel beside the bench. Behind Billy, Straw fires up her chainsaw. She finishes off the last section of a mountain ash. She piles the limbs into the drum, watches them stand tall and then collapse in sparks of ember.

"My father said to never run equipment before noon," Billy says to Straw.

"Billy. It's moonlight. Sound does not travel when nobody hears it."

"Oh," Billy says. Reluctantly, he puts his hearing aids in.

Slim Picker drives by. He beeps his horn. Billy sees that the rag-and-bone-man is happy. He marvels at how quickly Garbage Day comes around. A week becomes a minute; a minute becomes a second and a second, on the fly, escapes with a truck load of memories. Billy remembers his fox and then forgets the deer is gone, too. He hears a shish of steam. The industrial strength espresso machine growls and lifts off. He turns and watches Yeti decant a quick cup. He tamps out the grounds on Prometheus's knee and preps a new cup for Billy. A Canada goose appears out of nowhere and pecks the ground with its hard beak. Billy scoots it away with his foot.

Lord Bogroll flits from flower to flower. He hops out of his golf cart. Billy watches him plant a super tree seedling beside the stump of the mountain ash. He cups the tender thing with earth, stakes it with rebar and returns with a watering can from the back of his trailer. Lord B anticipates Billy's gaze. He looks up, shyly and locks his eyes in complete communion.

"Reforestation Billy!" Lord Bogroll says.

"Gentleness becomes you," Billy replies.

Billy pulls out a new reed and moistens it with his lips. He affixes it to his shawm. Billy inhales deeply, purses his lips like a prune and blows the opening notes of *"This is our music"* by Ornette Coleman. He hears a call of trumpet and Slim's drum responds. Stumblebum Waytes somehow perceives in advance each rehearsal.

Straw hefts her euphonium, tests the keys and lays down an odd rhythm made thicker by the breathy-giggles of Bogroll on clarinet. A long slide of trombone announces the late arrival of Two-Bits. Music climbs the peak and then swings headlong over the edge.

"Sleep in, Kid? "Billy laughs, in between whines on his shawm.

Two-Bits pauses and drains the gob out of his instrument. "It's a waistline thing, Pops. I went to the gym."

Billy stands now. Stumblebum Waytes falls in line. Slowly at first and then with increasing speed, the band circles Prometheus under the light of the waning Wolf Moon. Straw's burn barrel glows red and casts silhouettes of whirling creatures against cement. A swirl of motion lifts the Waytes like musical notes that linger in the air. Wind blows them down the south hill, over the four corners, past the Obsessa and deposits them at the base of the Cenotaph. Billy takes his bearings while the band checks their instruments.

VI

The Cenotaph stands vigil on a level patch at the bottom of a series of rising hills that support even rows of headstones. A canopy of trees sends shade, shadow and light-breezes to comfort moon-lit soldiers carved in stone. Billy feels the night breeze against his cheek and touches the square font of names etched in precise vertical rows. The sheer height of the statue dwarfs all the living things beside it; so much so that memory becomes a physical entity in-and-of-itself where the present bends her knee to the past and when she rises, she offers a prophesy of hope.

Billy appreciates fixed things not subject to change in the Bill-age. He prefers spaces not under new management. He knows permanence is a touchstone for meaning; a place where passion bursts forth from end, cause and the power of effect. Billy thinks it so odd that while a fixed thing is not static it still begets a possibility of constant change. At his age: (Bones creaking) History tells Billy more about where he is going than where he came from. Still, he picks out an old tune for Stumblebum Waytes to play under the light of the Wolf Moon.

"On four," Billy nods to Slim Picker who straightens his shoulders.

The drum rolls and punctuates the first eight bars of the march. The brass section joins in: Straw, then Yeti, then Two-Bits picks out the melody on valve trombone, slowly at first and then their tempo speeds up. The thin nasal whine of Billy's shawm creates an odd effect, almost as if a filament, or artery, something organic, flows through the entire song like blood. Billy leads the minstrels in circular fashion. Even though Stumblebum Waytes are the only souls present under the moonlight, Billy sees spirits march past him into the Cenotaph itself; or one by one, up the hills to blend into gravestone and marble. Billy hears whispers in his ears, like the ones inside of seashells. It surprises him when Slim Picker fades the last hurrah and his soft drumroll ends their rendition of *When Johnny Comes Marching Home*.

VII

The Last Micromoon

Billy drops straight down like a rock. He barely sees the moon shrink to a pinprick and when he lands, he lands with a thud. He stamps the ground with one foot to test reality. Billy turns a complete circle, orients himself and sees he is at a train station. He wonders if he leaves or arrives. He wonders if friends see him off of if he strains for friends-in-waiting. Billy knows what happens next. He denies it, the way he always does, and rolls his head back and forth in soft arcs of protest. A pillow cools his check. A yellow taxi cab pulls up. The back door opens and Billy's friend exits and walks past him. It amazes Billy that she didn't say hello. He turns and another friend runs past him and hops into the yellow taxi. The door slams shut. Billy looks for complete communion but this friend ignores his eyes. It stuns Billy that he did not bother to look. Billy begins to turn in circles but does not get dizzy. A train whistle sounds and he sits in the engine beside a Casey-Jones man who looks like his father and then his brother, then his father-in-law and then his mother-in-law and then his mother. Billy starts with his thumb and makes an effort to count the living from the dead. He tries to raise his index finger and his middle finger then his ring finger and then his baby finger but all he sees is thumb. Frantic, Billy switches hands to count his old friends but his thumb blocks further progress. The train pulls into a round house and the engine clicks around like a dial on a radio. Billy hears static, and snippets of a song he recognizes, but the song flips in and out of clarity, the more he tries to hear it.

"Billy. Please" Mrs. Hornpipe begs. "It's way too early. Why are you humming *Johnny Comes Marching Home*? Go to sleep, Baby."

"Everybody is changing," Billy says quietly.

"You are changing," Mrs. Hornpipe half-replies in the hypno-gogic dialect of mumble.

"It is odd to be alone," Billy whispers. He realizes the best confessions are in twilight, before thought outsmarts spirit.

"Honey? Put the espresso on. Go out and play today with the rest of the boys and girls, okay? I have to go to work soon."

"I will!" Billy replies. He reaches for his shawm and searches the nightstand again, for a new reed.

Worm Moon

Billy pulls in a breath, purses his lips and blows into his shawm. A beautifully thin, whine-y string of notes lifts up and disperses into the air. Two-Bits stops scrolling. He raises his head skyward and watches the melody get loft in sixteenth note sprinkles of pepper, across the lunar night.

"What the hell is a Worm Moon?" he asks out of the blue.

"It's how ancient people mark the seasons, you little Ape. The Worm Moon appears in March after the cold, hard geezis winter. Don't you get it? Smell the air. Feel the soft ground under your toes. The Billage is thawing; we all are. Spring is around the corner and the worms rise up to proclaim and renew. Look it up, Chum. There's an APP for it."

"Oh," Two-Bits replies. He bows his head and strokes his smart-phone in earnest.

I

Like Piltdown man, Billy walks erect now with free use of his hands. He pauses to inspect his palms and it pleases Billy to have the use of his counting fingers back. Or perhaps he rises from his sweat-stinky bed beside the Pool at Bethsaida. A disembodied voice proclaims he is out of the woods but should take it easy. Billy laughs at his flotsam jetsam jumble of thoughts *warshed* ashore like tangles of seaweed on the beaches at Billage twilight. He likes to say *warshed* as much as he likes to say Billage. A cormorant screeches, punctuates the atmosphere and dives at an impossible angle into a lake. Billy feels the hard, grainy beach sand under the soles of his feet and in the little pockets between his toes. Before he moves inland towards a hump of thick grass, he pauses to observe his toe-prints in the sand. A wave erases them completely. A breeze cools him and dissipates the fishy smells of water. The faint rind of horizon across the expanse catches Billy's gaze and then gravity pulls his eyes directly into the face of the Worm moon. The moon dominates the black slate of sky and highlights inky shapes of cloud the way a 2H pencil might. A vortex sucks Billy up. He ascends and sees his silhouette beside textures of crater and mountainside.

Billy shakes his head as if to re-set reality. He pulls at the drawstrings to cinch the waistline of his blue track pants. His sweatshirt smells fresh like lavender. Billy Hornpipe does the laundry on Sundays. He also keeps Mrs. Hornpipe and himself alive each week with a limited supper-time repertoire. Red meat disappears and lately the menu supplements with chicken, perch and leafy greens. It irks Billy. He misses his steak: (CC: Pill bottle rattles indignantly here).

Billy walks inland and feels the chill of dew-besotted grass under his feet. The smell of earth pervades his nostrils. Billy clicks his flashlight on and captures the glisten of dew worms. The earth releases them, grows warm and fertile and each creature stretches gloriously in the moonlight. Quick as lightning, Billy grabs one. The worm's speed surprises Billy and it slips back into its hole. Billy wipes the secretions on his track pants: (Rinse cycle clicking).

Billy knows that when the ground thaws, worms rise by the light of the moon and that spring is near. The variety store stacks cups of worms in Styrofoam stuffed with black earth in the drink cooler; but, tastefully, to the side. Billy captures another night crawler, inspects it and then returns it to the soil and her promise of fertility to come.

"Where are we playing today, Billy?" Straw calls out.

She stokes her burn barrel with a stick. The sprinkle of ember looks like red pepper in the air. The sparks could almost be notes of music made of light. Lord Bogroll hoses down Prometheus and Yeti fusses with the espresso machine. Slim Picker drives by on rounds and somewhere, Two-Bits rises like an earthworm, to the jingle of *Hail to the Chief* on his cell phone. He texts Stumblebum Waytes that he is on his way. Nobody receives the message for obvious reasons. The old stopped waiting around for the young, long ago. It was ever thus in the subjective tit-for-tat of misplaced urgency.

Billy sits beside Prometheus on the iron bench. He looks over the writer's shoulder and imagines what he writes on his little notepad. Moonlight illuminates Prometheus's script. Billy sees he finishes his manuscript and awaits word of its success. In the empathy of imagination, Billy beholds a pod of whales on the horizon. He lowers a dory into the sea and rows towards the pod. He puts his geezis back to the oars. A cold wave crashes over the bow. It chills Billy with excitement. Prometheus directs from the front. A Leviathan separates herself and undulates towards the horizon. Sun-kissed glistens give her away. A wave obscures her length and breadth but Billy sees the massive arch of her back and the barnacle-nubs on a fluke. Prometheus stands at-the-ready now; and as they overtake the great fish, he plunges a harpoon straight into her. The dory lurches, Prometheus and Billy tumble aft and a coil of rope spools out into a grey brine. Billy clutches the side of the dory. He hangs on while the boat corrects and then drags with resistance over peaks and troughs of waves. Full bore, line taut, the Leviathan sweeps them endlessly in what sailors call a Nantucket sleigh ride. Suddenly, the rope snaps, the dory comes to rest and then bobs insignificantly on the high literary seas. An overhead flutter of seagulls mocks them. Billy feels like a cork. "She has not given herself to us this time, Billy Hornpipe!" Prometheus cries.

"So you are reading a rejection letter on this bench?" Billy asks.

"No, ordering more harpoons," Prometheus replies.

A voice interrupts Billy's reverie:

"He's writing a cheque, Billy," Yeti calls out from beside the espresso machine. Yeti fingers his trumpet and lifts a tiny cup to his lips and blows. Intense caffeine soothes the savage beast, or at least, leaves a be-bop shiver of anticipation.

"It's the start of the month," the trumpeter reminds Billy. "Industrial strength espresso, remember? First installment for the receipt of small gratuities for services rendered. You've got to pay up to play up, Brother."

"It's too bad the Obsessa beat us out of our wet market," Lord Bogroll laments as he lifts his wand to water a pot of flowers on a lamp post. A piss of excess water splatters the concrete below.

A sound of a valve trombone interrupts the conversation. Billy swivels. He watches Two-Bit's shuffle over to the burn barrel. He sets his instrument down carefully and places his hands over the red globe of radiant warmth. "This baby has a nice draw. It's a masterpiece. You should patent it, Straw."

"What do we pay the mayor with, Yeti?" Billy interjects.

He pulls the pockets of his sweat pants inside out and lets them dangle.

"I don't carry cash and our pension cheque doesn't arrive until the end of the month."

"That's not a very good-look on you, Billy Hornpipe," Mrs. Hornpipe whispers out of the blue.

"Pay him with Bit-coin," Two-Bits says, matter-of-factly.

"How do I do that?" Billy asks.

Two-Bits looks at the Billy Hornpipe. "You really are a Billage Idiot, aren't you?"

Two-Bits stops, searches the ground and spots a cardboard hamburger container. He picks it up and tears a neat square from the top. Adeptly, he pulls out a small flat pen from his cell phone case. He hands the pen and the square of cardboard to Billy. "Just write .0000008, sign it, date it and let greed do the rest. I'll take a picture and send it electronically to the mayor: Done like dinner. We are all set for the Month of Worms, Billy."

Billy shakes his head. "We used to make our own pretend money as kids, Two-Bits. We were rich beyond our wildest dreams."

"The universe is overrated. It's the metaverse now, Pops."

"Meanwhile, on this earth, espresso is a lovesome thing, shithead." Billy laughs and takes his sip.

II

Billy knows the Worm moon still holds power over him. He feels the wax and wane of her grip, like spaces in-between pumps of his heart. He knows he is on the threshold of change. Billy feels glad to be rid of the asphalt road, with the cedars on the left and the silver ribbon of riber on the right; the cone of lamplight that points the way to the main drag of the Billage, but most of all, Billy feels happy his whirling dervish ceases and desists. He hates sweating so much and dislikes fruit cocktail ladled from fifty-gallon drums. A memory of industrial-strength mashed potatoes bursts through his taste buds onto the flat of his tongue. Billy licks his lips and pretends again, that he is a prisoner of war; how he savours, one ration at a time, the stainless-steel coffee in plastic cups; how everything was almost over before it even began. Billy Hornpipe captures and releases those thoughts now. Once and a while Billy gets the urge to spin and when the urge comes, he rocks his head against the pillow and gets dizzy; until Mrs. Hornpipe kicks his leg and tells him to stop it. When he awakens, his pillow feels cold again and moist from spittle. Somewhere in the twilight, a voice tells Billy that he is still not out of the woods just yet for his retiremento's heart is a pesky thing. You can never be too sure. He turns and reaches for his nightstand by rote. His fingers hop around the way a little sparrow pecks for seeds. Billy finds the reed and brings it to his mouth to moisten it. He tenderly fits the reed into his shawm. Evolved, he stands by his bedside and gazes adoringly at Mrs. Hornpipe. He refuses to play the instrument while his wife sleeps. Billy feels an illumination on his shoulders. Perspective changes and he gazes down now, while the light of the Worm Moon spills over him. His mind weaves through a spindly mass of maple branches and a dance of shadow flows through the window frame to part the blinds. Billy accepts the warm invitations of respiration. The gentle pulse of his heart comforts him, like familiar fire in Straw's burn barrel. His eyes widen: Quiet-as-a-mouse he stretches.

"Are you going for your walk today, Billy Hornpipe?" Mrs. Hornpipe whispers from their bed.

"Yes, I am," Billy says softly.

"Are you going out to play with your friends?"

"Yes, I am," Billy says and softly shuts the bedroom door. He makes a note to lubricate the squeak in the hinges.

Billy feels the warm globe of the burn barrel on his palms and then returns to his familiar spot beside Prometheus on the iron bench. He crosses his legs, ignores Two-Bits, turns to Straw and anticipates her question:

"Our first performance is south of the Billage, at the crossroads, where the country meets the shipping containers," Billy announces. "From there we make our way north along the main drag. Stumblebum Waytes is master and commander of her own ship. We play on our terms. We will beautify the Billage of Blight whether the mayor likes it or not. It is our civic duty; perhaps our destiny some might say. We decline all invitations to perform at council meetings and all 'Opening Soon' ceremonies: Let Bong Shops and tattoo parlours fall where they may. Stumblebum Waytes is going rogue."

"Don't forget milk and bread before you come home, Honey" Mrs. Hornpipe whispers.

III

Billy stands at the crossroads where the tired main drag ends and highway rushes south with abandon into the gridlock and conga lines of the city. He faces north and gazes past the car dealerships, the myriad flocks of urban Canada geese bathing in greasy mud puddles; past the big box stores to the right and the industrial wasteland on his left; past Prometheus, where his band loiters and sips espresso; past the walk-in clinic, the chain link fence and dueling parking lots on the miracle mile; down the hill, past the pop-up business to the four corners. He sees that Lord Bogroll faces off again, with yet another eighteen-wheeler. He refuses to budge. A siren sounds and suddenly, the air is starburst with intrusions of flashing red and pretty blue lights: an out-of-place Christmas reminder of criminal intent. Billy's gazes now through the core of the Billage; past the Obsessa on the right, the coffee shop across from it, the sub shops, tattoo parlours and the variety store that sells funky bongs. Billy notes the new cannabis shop occupies the space where Stumblebum Waytes hoped to start their wet market. He looks at the derelict restaurant, the River Pub that still cain't get the *kurri rite* (CC: teachers protest and write literary letters to town council, here), and then Billy's gaze stops on the bridge where the long road leads to the streetlamp and the river-road between the cedars on the right and the silver ribbon of riber on the left. What a laugh: really.

Billy sighs the way an older man sighs at the sight of his naked body in a mirror.

"It is time to tidy up," he whispers to himself.

Mrs. Hornpipe suddenly appears. She throws her arms around Billy's image. "Let's tidy up together," she laughs like wind-in-their-chimes.

Billy returns now to the threshold of the Billage. The Shipping Yard grows exponentially like cancer, just inside the Billage line, and then the wound leaks with pus-y abandon south, past Al's Big Tires. A yellow bulldozer flattens the corn, corn, corn field across the road to make way for a million square feet of mail-order warehouse.

"Only a fool stands in line when he can order online" says a self-satisfied Billboard to "We": the people.

A seagull holds court and watches a man with an orange hard hat drop a crust of peanut butter sandwich and step on it. A hawk lifts off, and disappears to the north where cancer and country cannot comingle. When a citizen approaches Blight from the south, she prays she is not delayed by a red light, for her interminable wait affronts all dignity at the threshold of the Billage. Inertia forces each soul to bear witness to the holy eyesore that acts as gateway to community—like a shitty pig-of-a-neighbour who spews refuse, out of sight/out of mind at the back of his/her/its property and smack-dab on the doorstep of Blight. Piltdown men and women still … walk … among us.

Billy licks the reed, fastens it to his shawm and lifts the instrument to his lips. Around and amidst him, an unruly flurry of tweaks, honks, blats, arpeggios, warbles and muffles signals the intentional dither of tuning; the wild promise of pre-music and melodies yet to come.

Stumblebum Waytes stands dwarf-like amidst the towers of orange corrugated shipping containers that surround them like opera boxes in a cavernous space. Is it not all urban theatre?

Cold radiates from the dark rolling pockets of corrugated sheets of steel against Billy's cheeks. He shivers. The Worm Moon shines innerlit in a full glory of night-glow. Her twilight majesty creates a small stage and her rays cast shadows upon the serenaders. A silhouette blends their shape together like a mountain range. A mouse skitters across the limelight and searches for a concealed spot from which to watch. Solemnly, Slim Picker begins a tom-tom repetition of beats and Billy feels sonorousness inside his chest.

"Let's do *Walls Come Tumbling Down*," Billy says. "On three..."

He breathes in, purses his lips like a prune and blows. One by one each instrument enters the melody; first the trumpet, then the euphonium, then the valve trombone and then finally, Lord B's clarinet augments and chases the whine-y melody of Billy's shawm like a squirrel up a tree. Slim is in the drummer's pocket and keeps time. The music rises into the moist night-air and somehow feels oddly pungent, like smells of antiseptic in Billy's nostrils. Trance-like, Stumblebum Waytes begins to turn in a circle, slowly at first and then with increasing speed. The face of the Worm-y moon appears then disappears and soon melts into a buttery rush of light. At the height of the vortex, Billy signals the last chorus, Stumblebum Waytes ceases to play, and abruptly the sound of crickets replaces silence.

"They play better than us!" Straw laughs. She has a right to laugh for she is the only true musician in the bunch.

Slim Pickens lifts his drum into the back of his pick-up. As if on air, he hops into the cab, slams the door and starts the engine. The band piles in, all except Two-Bits: Billy rides shotgun.

"Where to Billy?" Slim says.

"To the car dealerships!" Billy replies.

"What about me?" Two-Bits asks.

"Text us when you get there, Bub," Yeti calls out.

A chime of *Hail to the Chief* twinkles on Two-Bit's smart phone. He takes the call, ignores Stumblebum Waytes completely and orders 300 dollars' worth of Bit-coin. Satisfied; nay, slightly distracted, he hangs up and tracks red tail-lights north, to a row of car dealerships.

IV

By a trick of twilight, the first car dealership looms into view like a lost marina of bobbing ships. Perhaps it would be clever to say they saw a death's head 'Jolly Roger' but the pirate flag does not exist in Blight; only perhaps the white flag of surrender. A Canada goose waddles in-between two SUVs and snuggles onto her nest. When Billy acclimatizes his eyes, the entire lot shuffles with birds in sensible blue suits, temporary license plates and rings of keys. Two-Bits arrives and a goose offers to sell him a used car. Crypto-currency confuses the bird. Earthbound, it lives, has no pension and has to get by. Two-Bits rolls his eyes, kicks a tire and takes another call on his smartphone: Youth is an urgent thing.

A five-pound bag of sunflower seeds rips open. Each gander squawks and squabbles around pebbles of food that spill between cars. Stumblebum Waytes stands in 'hep' repose with instruments at the ready. Each musician slouches, in the *smoke 'em if you got 'em*, Cool-Cat attitude of the jazz-besotted. Billy knows he could murder a cigarette; perhaps they all could. He licks the reed of his shawm and signals his serenaders in for the count. Pride fills Billy's heart. He realizes they play pro bono; not for the mayor; not for bong shops, tattoo parlours, derelict buildings and foreclosures; but for a currency of intimate meaning in a reward full of purpose. Billy Hornpipe plays for new things now. He no longer hand-wrings over things that are lost.

"Why do you wear the same clothes every day, Billy?" Mrs. Hornpipe says sleepily.

"This is my uniform now. Easier to wash," Billy replies, slightly irked.

"You smell like smoke, Honey": (Spin-cycle starts again).

Billy's shawm lifts melody like a sensuous snake rising out of a basket made of corn, corn, corn husk or something. The group joins in. A cluster of notes mist the air the way a hose rinses dust from cars to make them shiny before the customers' come. They play *Stella by Starlight.*

Stumblebum Waytes laughs after the song ends. Lord Bogroll breaks down his clarinet into three parts. His method starts a chain reaction with the other musicians. Darkness paints the clouds. An alpha goose stutter steps, flaps her wings and gets loft in the twilight. Soon the entire flock joins him/her/us; scattered at first and then their beautiful pattern takes shape. The formation sweeps north in perfect silhouette across the face of the Worm Moon; it gathers its urban friends from mud puddles and parking lots along the way. Swiftly, like balloons rising, the gaggle bunches and travels south to the threshold of Blight. The formation searches for imaginary corn, corn, corn that sprouts resolutely in reclaimed fields to refresh the land.

"Time for espresso!" Yeti yells to break the reverie.

Slim Picker fires up the pick-up, Two-Bits hops in the back and quick-as-a-bunny, Stumblebum Waytes warms their hands atop the rosy-red glow of burn barrel to await small pleasures of steamy black joy. Billy chats with Prometheus on his iron bench.

V

"Prometheus is writing you a ticket for loitering, Billy," Yeti teases. "Why do you spend so much time with the statue?"

"I love what she stands for," Billy whispers silently.

"He's sitting, Pops," Two-Bits says smugly.

"Will you always be a shithead?" Billy says to the young man.

"Youth is a lovesome thing," the Boy replies wistfully.

(CC: Two-Bits bares his teeth and tears the cellophane off a complimentary biscotti he lifted from the car dealership. He intends to dunk and the other go to hell.)

Straw picks up an empty cigarette pack and writes '.00000008' on it.

"Watch this, Kid," she says, and then drops it into the fire.

"How could you?" Two-Bits howls.

The statue of the writer is next to the miracle mile so Billy takes the band a dozen yards south; past the walk-in clinic, the burger shop, the sub shop, the nail shop, Peet's Peetzah and two greasy fish and chips joints. The *BiRite/DiWel* discount store snoozes beside a phone booth that nobody remembers how to use anyway. The phone booth stands vigil beside The Lard, one of Blight's many sports bars, so called; where chubby citizens wear baseball caps backwards and shnibble chicken wings to yummy eternity.

Billy gazes across the main drag at the mirror image on the other side. He knows there is not much Stumblebum Waytes can do for the miracle mile but he gestures for the band to set up on the asphalt boulevard. Billy notes there is not a blade of grass to be seen anywhere in the moonlight.

Lord Bogroll anticipates Billy's thoughts: "This is barren land, Lord B."

Lord B opens his hands at the waist: "I'm working on it," the gardener replies. "I'll put planters; there, there and there … like urban corn, corn, corn, Billy."

Billy watches Straw collect garbage for her burn barrel and then she joins the serenaders, inserts the mouthpiece in her euphonium, shifts its weight and tests its keys. Silently Two-Bits glides his slide, Lord Bogroll adjusts his reed, Slim Picker positions his drum mallets comfortably and Billy aligns his fingertips with the holes on his shawm. Like a bandleader, Billy gestures to Yeti to count them in. Yeti lifts his trumpet skyward and just as he brings it down on the beat, Stumblebum Waytes hears another band start up across the road. The band sounds fuller and richer than Billy Hornpipe's. Billy sees they have two of every instrument, including a cello, and that they are well turned out in blue uniforms, gold buttons with red stripes on the legs. Each of them wears an officer's cap. Billy turns to his own band and thinks for the first time it may be time to get out of sweatpants and tidy up. He gestures to Yeti and soon the miracle mile fills with a beautiful trumpet call and response, back and forth across the road: (CC: *Quiet City* by Aaron Copeland plays here). Slowly Stumblebum Waytes circles in the moonlight. Their speed increases and the Worm Moon blends into butter again. Billy hears the tintinnabulation of chimes and the shimmer of a simple chrome triangle. Its silver ting-a-ling pierces the twilight. Billy loves the counterpoint to the brass, the booming percussion and the whine of his shawm. When the song ends, Billy looks up in primitive homage to the face of the Worm moon. A lone goose flies by; punctuates the sky and it actually feels like a black and white commercial on tee bee: the last of the urban stragglers exits Blight and heads north for a better habitat before the test pattern crackle of static at midnight—Oh geezis—about a hundred or so years ago when things were stable, permanent, dependable; maybe even healthy in the Billage.

Silently, Billy ambles across the road to talk with the other musicians. He feels the easy kinship musicians feel. The bandleader pulls on a cigarette, drops it on the ground and smears it with her foot.

"We don't have a shawm in our band," she says. You should come over and sit in with us. We don't play for the mayor either. Ours is a greater good."

"Billy? The library is looking for book shelve-ers. You should volunteer. Put some meaning in your life. You lust after books, don't you? I put the article by your chair," Mrs. Hornpipes says.

"It is a pleasure to meet you," Billy Hornpipe says to the bandleader and her band.

He turns, crosses the road and enjoys the clack, clatter and kibbutz as Stumblebum Waytes dismantles their instruments.

"What did the bandleader say, Billy?" Straw asks.

"She said our trombone section sucks," Billy replies.

"No way!" Two-Bits squawks and looks around for support.

"With the number of shipping containers shrinking, she said the gateway to the Billage looks better: With the geese leaving for reclaimed corn, corn, corn fields, new stores will come to beautify Blight: specialty stores, international food markets, Thai joints and authentic curry emporiums … that kind of stuff."

"Jamaican curry?" Yeti asks out loud.

"Blight will be a Billage then and not an ersatz enclave!" Lord Bogroll laughs.

"Exactly!" Billy says.

"Where do we play next Billy Hornpipe?" Straw asks.

Billy pauses and looks into the full face of the Worm Moon. He knows time rushes now.

"Let's assemble downtown, in front of the Obsessa," he replies. "We can work it out from there."

"I'll get the truck," Slim Picker says and then disappears into the twilight.

"Can you find us a cello, Slim?" Billy asks.

Micromoon (slight return)

Billy climbs into bed and throws his arm around Mrs. Hornpipe's ridgeline under the covers. He savours the touch of intimacy, of love-lived-long. His libido changes and Billy notes at this season of his life that, perhaps, cuddling is passion at parade-rest. The pageantry never leaves and Billy loves the warm feel of the whirls of his fingertips upon the whirls of her fingertips. Fortune blends all deep recesses on their lunar palms. A sigh replaces a moan surely in the land of sleepyheads. Billy appreciates that all flags still stand at attention for her and her only, on the parade ground most days not all; anyways and the other so what. Youth is a wistful thing. (CC: sigh here).

"All that glitters is not gold," Billy whispers to Mrs. Hornpipe's neck.

"Focus on the gold, Honey," Mrs. Hornpipe mumbles and then departs from this earth.

Billy rolls onto his back and thinks. He does not play-dead anymore. It does not even cross his geezis mind. He peers outside of the frame of the bedroom window like a normal boy. It surprises him that that there is no micromoon anymore; only stars with tree branches in the foreground. There is no midground and maybe the background informs, but really doesn't matter now. It is hard to know: Billy does not have the monopoly on truth. He did once, when he was young.

He thinks and he thinks and soon he forgets what he thinks and flutters through the space of pre-dream into the depths of actual dreams. Anxiety enters Billy through a pressure on his bladder. He fights it and suddenly appears at a desk inside a campus with green blackboards and creamy yellow chalk. It amazes Billy that he now finds the class that he never finds in his Bermuda Triangle of searching. Impossibly, Yeti sits beside him on the journey. Observation replaces his trumpet. His hands are free to learn.

Billy loves calculus: the symbols, her order, the game; the deeper equations of mathematical meaning. He loves green chalkboards. He loves $X + Y = L$ to the exponent n, where L = love. Billy sees the creamy-white outline of an isosceles triangle on the board: S is at the apex and BH is at the base on the left with a representative R for relationship on the right (where R is a placeholder for MH: Mrs. Hornpipe, period). Somebody bangs the oblong brush and chalk dust fills the stupid twilight classroom of recurring dreams. The geezis dust settles and Billy Hornpipe sees that as BH ascends, and concordantly, the value of R ascends; there is a lessening of distance within the area of the triangle between he and the astronomical value of MH. Slowly they approach the pinnacle of S where S = the Ideal.

"I could murder a steak," Billy whispers to Yeti.

Yeti guffaws.

"You might want to replace S with something more ideal, shithead," he says.

"All my relationships changed, Yeti."

"Why do you persist on hand-wringing this?"

"Am I getting older?" Billy asks.

"Change changes regardless. She waits for you to catch up," The Yeti whispers.

"I can control space," Billy says defensively.

"You cannot control time, Bub," Yeti replies.

"I have always tried to control time," Billy says.

"Get over it, Kid."

"Am I not still young, like Two-Bits?" Billy pleads.

"What does your body tell you?" Yeti replies resolutely.

Billy ignores the question.

"I lost a lot of friends when I retired, Yeti," Billy confesses.

Yeti gestures to the green chalkboard.

"We are all ascending our own triangles, Billy Hornpipe. Make new friends, Brother. Your old friends have a place in time and celebrate the sacredness of that. We are all allowed to change musicians and bands, or are you that naïve?"

"Should I purchase a smartphone?" Billy asks urgently.

"Are you kidding me?" Yeti replies with disgust.

"Ding, ding, ding." A bell rings. Billy actually geezis hears the harsh tintinnabulation of it. There is no close caption. The life-long twelve rounds are over and done with. Yeti's chair scrapes back in the kerfuffle. He stands beside Billy and gently says:

"I got a new letter at the top of my triangle, Billy. It's time I leave Stumblebum Waytes."

"It is a pleasure to meet you," Billy says at a loss for words.

Billy finds himself on the south hill. He sits beside Prometheus now and imagines the iron-writer sketches an isosceles triangle on his iron note pad. Water drips from over-hanging plants, recently watered, nearby. There is an absence of bird-lime on the bench.

A strobe of flashing red/blue light coats Billy's face. How can this be? It is nowhere near the moon of Christmas. He looks up and sees a police officer glide by in the stillness of twilight. Billy knows she heads north, down the hill to the four corners. He hears the bowel-rumble of an eighteen-wheeler and suspects *thar's trouble* in the valley.

Slim Picker pulls to the curb.

"You're late, Billy. Hop in." he says.

Slim drives north down the hill. He gives the eighteen-wheeler a wide birth, signals and turns right on the road that leads to Serenity Acres. Billy sees Lord Bogroll, in full-blown Tiananmen Boggy mode. Steadfast: He refuses to let the truck advance. The cop is already out of her vehicle. She beaches the car at an odd angle and blocks traffic with a seasoned mixture of entitlement-to-power and a veiled contempt for citizen tomfoolery. Judgement made; she reaches for her citation pad.

Billy rolls down the window in the cab.

"We have got to put an end to this once and for all, Billy," Lord Bogroll yells.

"Hang on," Billy shouts back.

Slim parks the pick up around the corner of the abandoned fish shop. Billy hops out of the cab and approaches the crossroads. Slim follows with his drum. Billy turns the corner and sees Stumblebum Waytes assembled in front of the Obsessa. Straw cues the serenaders and waits for Billy to put his shawm together.

VI

Billy moistens his reed and makes ready. Lord Bogroll pisses off the truck driver who exits his rig and prepares to smack him. Nobody gives a shit anymore. The cop intervenes the way cops do and she uses the full threat of the possibility of jail time. As if to punctuate her point, the police cruiser light flashes blue and red and now, even white like a moon; blue and red and now, even white like a moon; blue and red and now, even white like a moon, in the twilight. Billy hears sirens in the spaces in-between the strobe. The siren aches to be turned on; to create a spectacle; to herald the presence of fools; but even the cop knows it is too early to go full bore on the thing. Lord Bogroll enters the crime scene chin-first and clearly wants the confrontation; in fact, he lives for it. Billy Hornpipe loves his commitment: If fisty-cuff it be, Billy has his boy's back but to be honest it hurts to be smacked on the chin.

Straw prepares Stumblebum Waytes for the next song. She signals Billy to count the band in.

"Now would be a good time to play, Billy. Where is Yeti?" Straw asks.

Billy pauses.

"Yeti solved the equation. G is for grandfather at the apex. He leaves us, never to return."

"I can play the trumpet parts, Billy. We'll get by. Your hand-wringing days are over."

Billy purses his lips. He fills his lungs and blows into the reed of his shawm. He charms the urban snake with a rush of whine-y notes. The snake pushes the top of its basket off and like an erect silver ribbon of riber, sways slowly in the din. The serpent poises to strike; completely pissed off. She fills each eye, yellow, with poison and where there is poison there is rage. It stuns Billy to observe the coils of his malevolence. He remembers his sessions on mindfulness at the hospital and gathers in deep air, prunes his lips and exhales with resolve into his instrument.

Straw comes in next on euphonium. Musician to the end, she plays on the upper register to approximate Yeti's trumpet bursts. Slim Picker realizes they move into a funky rendition of *Downtown* and picks up the tempo on drum. Two-Bits soars then on valve trombone, and nails the first solo, the bridge and then the chorus. He fills the gaps of Bogroll's unbridled hyena-laugh on clarinet. Stumblebum Waytes turns and turns and feels swing within their dervish. The monotonous strobe of police light dilutes the butter-blur of moon ray. This irks Billy at first but he resolves the tension. He craves reality now and not the miserable pities of an applied psychosis of dreams.

The song ends. The flashing strobe of the police cruiser amplifies silence and carries the beat, expectantly, into the musical rests of twilight, like stupid pepper but you can't see pepper in night air. How boring it gets to see something that is not there.

Straw loves the installation art effect of instruments and car. So does Slim Picker. They are what we call artists, after all.

"I am going to look for a strobe light now, Billy Hornpipe," the Rag-and-bone-man says. "It's very *Edgar Varese*. Stumblebum Waytes needs more percussion."

It impresses Billy that Slim even knows who Edgar Varese is. Nobody does any more but for some reason, he disagrees with the use of a strobe light in the music of the Waytes.

Billy feels melancholy as he removes the reed from his shawm. The revolving light triggers him.

"It reminds me of an ambulance, Straw," Billy confesses.

"Noting same," Straw says. She comes over and frankly, hugs Billy with an intimacy of understanding. "You're healthy now, Bub!" She laughs the laugh-of-chimes and chases Billy's fever like a girl up a rope ladder into the clouds.

In the aftermath of twilight crimes, the police officer writes the eighteen-wheeler up for a citation. Everyone's "asshole meter" is re-calibrated, is the collective point. Nobody sees when justice is done in moonlight for it is approximate yet expected. Life is quiet like dat, dat and datly dat on the snare of resolve. The officer talks peacefully with Lord Bogroll the way cops do when they pass urban judgement and take sides with citizens.

Billy comes to Lord B's side and sees the Gardener from Belize is also at peace.

The cop allows the truck driver to turn right at the crossroads and invites her to surely make her-way-the-hell-out of the Billage of Blight *toot suite*. Disgruntled, the rig roars, waddles, settles, passes wind, grinds-gear and heads east towards Serenity Acres; past the little after-thought of a sister-town, to escape towards a freedom full-bore on the highway.

"Billy?" Lord Bogroll confides. "I am ready to leave Stumblebum Waytes. The trucks will use the bypass and I can concentrate on watering my plants. You are the ultimate bandleader and I loved playing with you and Slim and Straw, Yeti and Two-Bits.

"It is a pleasure to meet you," Billy replies.

Slim Picker hefts his drum into the back of his pickup. *Hail to the Chief* lights up Two-Bit's smartphone: He stoops his head in millennial worship and takes the call. Straw grows antsy and says she needs to walk away and burn shit.

Billy beholds his friends. Moonlight becomes them. It leaves them stan-ding, a-lone, after all. Sunlight slides unannounced yet subtle into the mix of dew and darkness. Somewhat overdue, Billy Hornpipe feels beautiful inside. Lung's work, heart beats, love exists, and the flagstaff flies fealty so what else is there? He raises his eyes and looks full into the Worm Moon.

"I could murder a hit of caffeine," Billy says to Stumblebum Waytes. "Meet me at Prometheus and we'll plan our next gig: Slim. Fire up the espresso machine, okay?"

"Roger that Billy," Slim replies loyally. He leaves the Obsessa, turns the corner and makes way for the abandoned fish market to retrieve his pick-up truck. Straw follows and calls to Two-Bits, who lifts his head, looks disoriented and stumbles after the serenaders.

Billy takes a glorious moment to himself. He turns and peers into the Oracle of the Obsessa. Light glows through the broad window. Somewhere in the back, Billy spots a plume of cigarette smoke: The *Haversham Reno Company* sets up for the eternal day. It is all renovation, frankly.

Pink Moon

(Billy makes peace with time)

Billy integrates foreground, midground and background and takes his time observing. Once again, he realizes what a gift of perspective it is to see his exterior, his interior and vague reflections of his future all at once. He uses the word *bague* instead of vague and laughs at the silliness of billage-words. Billy walks upright and reminds himself he is healthy again. He shed his tail and could care less now.

"It is a pleasure to meet you," he says to the reflection on his window pane.

Billy places his hand on his jaw and turns his face right and then left. It is a man's testosterone motion and Billy knows he is overdue for a shave. Billy gazes down. He sees his waistline and sucks his tummy in. It is a man's vanity and Billy knows he needs to walk more; not the dervish walks, but real walks in real time. Finally, Billy sees both hands pluck and pull out the slack of his sweatpants before the mirror. It is a man's complacency and after all, Mrs. Hornpipe still thinks he's a sexy shpring chicken. Billy rejects ties, belts and suit pants, head, thorax and abdomen, and no longer wishes to be held together like a worker bee. He pollinates only dreams now. He embraces his freedoms. He finds meaning: He leads Stumblebum Waytes and in their heyday, they nailed it.

The new knowledge pushes Billy Hornpipe's gaze through the glass of the window into the recesses of the Obsessa. Once again, he observes the curious *'fish tank'* phenomenon of workers in the midst of their useful toil; floating, darting, resting their fins, unaware of observance from without. Gills puffing. Billy lusts after a cigarette but replaces the craving with a more *senstible* desire for caffeine. Billy likes to say *senstible* like 'Piggy' in *Lord of the Flies*. He knows *it is better to be more senstible like 'Ralph', than a bunch of painted savages.* He loves that book. He loves books, period, and lines them up perfectly on library shelves in his mind, like music in rows; like jazz unrestrained by form yet waiting to be heard. Words have as much pepper as notes in the air. (CC: laugh with me here, Bub).

The *Haversham* renovations are eternal but Billy sees they are farther along from the last time he looks. Who knows when they will finish and who knows what the meaning and purpose of this store will be? It dawns on Billy Hornpipe that much like the Obsessa, the timetable of his own completion is up for grabs and the other so what.

Billy loses himself in reverie and gets what Yeti calls *milk eyes*: That far-off stare that his granddaughter gets when she feeds and becomes so content, she swoons. Billy swoons and his eyes sigh and his sigh opens up memories into mysterious nooks and crannies and drywall and dust, ripples of metal corrugations and a hammer lying around and other distractions of rapture:

Somewhere, in a country to the south, Billy Hornpipe enters a cenote with twenty other *tourisimmi*. Mrs. Hornpipe holds Billy's hand. They are retired after all. Billy gazes at her fingers; maybe first, their ring finger: He actually feels the contour of whirls, the hills and valleys of micro love. He loves the warm butter-glow of gold which minds its own business now, stays precious and exists now, without fanfare, the way respiration animates lungs, now. Billy takes in the moist (fetid frankly tourist) air of the cave and hears the plink of water in pools beside stepping stones. He loves that he and Mrs. Hornpipe bring up the rear of the tour; for the last becomes the first to exit the unknown. Billy ducks when the group descends. He pauses to touch rock with his fingertips. Rocks possess texture. Nobody knows. At the end of the pathway, the cave opens into a cavern and a candle illuminates an old man in white. Billy's lip curls for it feels touristy in the key of ersatz. Money buys approximations of reality; after all, don't it? Mrs. Hornpipe shushes Billy; tells him to stop his running commentary and just experience the damn thing, Honey Bun. Billy listens (CC: as best he can). Billy watches and for once; he stops hand-wringing the thing to death. He stands reverently in a circle, lives in the moment and like the rest of the twenty-dollar-a-head, tourists, Billy allows himself to be really purified on vacation. The group turns and Billy leads the way with Mrs. Hornpipe into the future. When they emerge into the sunlight, the tour guide gives them the rest of the afternoon to explore. Mrs. Hornpipe pauses. She steps off the trail, pulls Billy behind ancient walls and enchanted hieroglyphics and they kiss. Well now, and Ho now and Yay now.

The warmth on his lips brings Billy's sight back from past into the present: Frankly, for the first time in a long time, he focuses. He spots the lamplight in the interior of the Obsessa, raises his eyes and observes how the Pink Moon's reflection shines rosy on the glass window in front of his nose.

"You have good colour this morning, Billy," Mrs. Hornpipe murmurs and then rolls over.

Billy smiles and kisses his wife's head. He loves the scent of her hair. He rises and the aromas of espresso and burning wood replace the sweet lavender in his nostrils. Billy sits on a hard bench, feels the iron skin of Prometheus somehow warm his shoulder but grows weary now, of moons and of moonlight.

Straw tenderly hands Billy an espresso. Slim tinkers with straps on his trailer and tightens down a brass headrail and bed frame. Two-Bits leans against the wall of the walk-in clinic and catches his second sleep.

"Where do we play next, Billy?" Straw calls out.

Billy brings the espresso to his nostrils and pulls the steam in through his nose. He closes his eyes and lifts his head. "In the heart of the Billage, my friends!"

"I'll play the clarinet part," Two-Bits volunteers.

The cab door slams and Slim Picker starts up his truck.

II

Slim Picker pulls up to the curb in front of the dead roadhouse beside the Mortgage & Loan building on the main drag. The dead roadhouse is dusty, dry and decrepit; like an old man in a wheel-chair. Time pushes the frame's shoulders down and the structure slumps to the left, like puree overcooked in a Teflon pan. Brown paper covers the windows and between cover and dust, the glassy stare leaves a perception of eyes gone rheumy. A pad lock on the door denies entry: no way in and no way out, although Billy notes cement footings, underneath, where the foundation crumbles in-ward. He smells exhalations of rot and mildew and steps back.

Billy remembers long ago, this carcass of wood was a watering hole populated by an odd mix of Billage parents with their chil-dren, tourists en route to cottages in the north, and bikers with broad backs and strong wishes to be left in peace. Everything works within spaces of acceptance and good cheer. Billy sees chil-dren pretend to wait on tables. Speechless, a little girl stands and watches a family eat. A father smiles and offers the little girl a copper bit-coin. She clutches it, beams and returns to her parent's table convinced, wide-eyed, that every moment of *can't believe, make-believe*, is true.

Billy sees that the abandoned space is nothing now. He decides it is the right place for Stumblebum Waytes to play. Billy wants to purify it. He signals Straw. Straw stops prying a board for her burn barrel; sets her crowbar down and gently places her mouth piece into the euphonium. Two-Bits rests his valve trombone on his left shoulder and tests the slide. Slim straightens his back, shuffles and settles his drum into place. Stumblebum Waytes looks at Billy poised to play. He feels complete communion. Billy moistens the reed of his shawm and inserts it into the body of the instrument. He touches the end of the bell, feels the shawm's heft, shrugs his shoulders and raises his arms to come in on the down-beat.

The band of serenaders plays an old eighties tune called *Rise Up*. Slim Picker's boom-bah drum solo claims the song and makes it theirs. Music spins the Waytes, slowly at first and then with in-creasing speed. Billy Hornpipe catches the Pink Moon out of the corner of his eye; but easily dismisses it. He integrates the whirl of his dervish. He experiences it now, as a threshold into a new way of thinking. He feels stronger. Stumblebum Waytes forgets about Lord Bogroll and The Yeti. Nobody misses them. Improvisation fills the spaces and rhythm fills time with an urgency to see now, to be now, and to live now.

Across the road, the marquee on the pub near the river twinkles like a micromoon:

"Under New Management. Come One. Come All … to the Fox and Doe-Head. Try our curry. We get it EXACTLY right!"

Billy makes a note to bring Mrs. Hornpipe around on a date. He knows it's been too long since they dated. Mrs. Hornpipe waits patiently to be asked. She possesses a woman's wisdom; for her heart speaks directly through her thoughts and offers an unlimited understanding; but only to men who listen.

Straw takes off on her solo. She sweeps Stumblebum Waytes back into a groove and her swing punctuates the twilight with a gossamer flurry of light-notes. High in a pot on a lamp post, a flower shrugs off the laden drop of chilly dew; stretches her yellow petals and bops. Billy watches every flower straighten the way a sunflower in a field turns eastward like a choir of broad sunny faces. Billy turns and the Fox & the Doe-Head disappears from his mind. He focusses while Slim Picker plays visions of a treasure beyond. The dead roadhouse shimmers like a mirage and then melts into nothing and from that nothing, a new structure rises. It shines like an imaginary gold Bit-coin, somewhere in the clouds. Slim Picker furls his brow. Billy Hornpipe watches him scale a sturdy ladder and finish printing *"Bin Around the Block"* on a sign under the apex of his new store. "I" is for ideal and Slim Picker ascends to the tip of his triangle. A fleet of pick-up trucks with trailers lines up at the curb. Carefully, Slim selects each treasure and carries it tenderly across the threshold of *Bin Around the Block*. He steps with greater meaning now and his passion humbles Billy Hornpipe. Slim finds homes for the discarded collections of all the retired men and woman in the Billage of Blight. Every Monday he finds things their children find no value in. Slim resolves the chord between must-have and don-t need. Billy feels feather-lite like a 40 foot ladder at a hardware store. He knows it is not from fever but from joy. He releases the gravity of the moon, ascends and realizes it is only about dreams now. He wants to purge everything he collects and be free of baggage. Billy bequeaths everything to his rag and bone man.

Billy Hornpipe breathes in, purses his lips like a prune and takes Stumblebum Waytes' last, sweet solo. A stream of notes pours out of his shawm like a silver ribbon. A snake appears and then another snake and another snake. Their coiled motion fascinates Billy. The knot of creatures flicks their tongue in unison. A wave forms. It undulates like a sine curve that carries the collective serpent up the hill, out of the Billage and into to the safety of the Wetlands to the north.

Stumblebum Waytes finishes on the beat and again lets silence take over. Slim Picker stretches his back and removes his beautiful drum. Smiling, he approaches Billy, Straw and Two-Bits.

"Billy. I have to go now. I'm leaving Stumblebum Waytes."

"It is a pleasure to meet you," Billy replies wistfully.

Slim loads the drum into the back of his pick-up truck. He tests the hitch on the trailer. A truck door opens and bangs shut with resolve. An engine turns over and growls. Slim steps on the accelerator and signals to head north into the twilight. He beeps *Shave and a Hair Cut: Ten Cents!* on the horn. Billy laughs at the joke and Slim Picker leaves with the blessings of the Pink Moon.

Hail to the Chief interrupts the moment. Two-Bits bows his head in immediate homage, takes the call and passes the smartphone to Billy.

"It's the mayor, Billy. He sounds pissed."

Billy pulls his hearing aid out and places the phone next to his ear.

"Where's my rent money, shithead? It's the start of the month remember?"

Billy turns to Two-Bits and covers the phone. "I thought you paid him?" Billy says.

"I did!" Two-Bits replies.

Billy hands the smart phone back to Two-Bits in disgust. "Work it out, Kid."

Equipment packed, Straw walks south with Billy towards the statue of the writer, her burn barrel and the industrial strength espresso machine. Billy turns. He spots Two-Bits under a cone of lamplight. With shoulders stooped and head cocked his right-hand gestures wildly in the night.

"Meet us at the Statue, Kid!" Billy shouts.

III

Before they arrive at the four corners and walk up the south hill, Billy catches sight of his image in the window of the Obsessa. Straw notices and stops to stand with him, slightly out of view.

The silent motion inside attracts Billy again and he turns to look inward. Before he looks deeper, Billy catches the last reflection of the Pink Moon off the window pane. The moon tires of him now but takes a moment and pays homage to his presence. Billy Hornpipe feels pink. He no longer dreams the recurrent dreams and his actual dreams are just garden-variety like Lord Bogroll's twilight watering of plants in the Billage. Billy wonders how much of his life, even before the white sheets and prisoner-of-war coffee, arose out of fever. He turns and gazes into the aquarium that is the Obsessa. Light softens the interior, almost with tenderness, and Billy loves the degrees of light, frankly: the unforgiving brightness of the sun, the gentle beckoning's of starlight, the pale anonymous gaze of the moon. Billy realizes as he looks, that nobody looks. Billy catches himself and corrects his calculus. Love looks. Mrs. Hornpipe looks and he looks at Mrs. Hornpipe. "Love looks," Billy nods to himself and the resolute silence completes his equation like a chalkboard in an empty classroom.

A *Haversham's Reno*-worker busies himself in the interior. Like all construction, until it finishes, it will never be complete. Billy feels content to simply observe and poke fun at words: *Everyting* is a work in progress: what is fixed is later in need of repair where t = time. Of course, Billy Hornpipe still craves cigarettes. He wants to be a drywaller when he grows up and lusts after plumes of smoke. The daydream gives way to another trance of *milk eyes* and Billy knows he is well-fed now, by peace. Billy shifts his sight and observes his reflection in the window. He feels the slight chill of ghosts and then the warmth of Straw's presence near him. His nose reacts to a violation of musk; released somewhere to saturate each molecule of air. Despite the presence of a peculiar odour, Billy realizes that there is so much going on now; that there is so much to do. All that glitters is not gold and Billy knows he is not perfect. A green blackboard replaces the sheen of the Obsessa Window. Chalk dust clouds the air. Billy traces an isosceles triangle with his fingertip; puts his own values at the base and puts his own value upon the apex. He begins his feather-lite climb again with Mrs. Hornpipe. He remembers the push of his past and beholds the invitations to his future. Billy steadies himself. He bundles up his applied psychosis together with his blue gown and paper slippers, arcs his arms and shoots a three-pointer into an industrial strength laundry hamper. For a split-second he is naked until he finds his sweatpants but for the first time in that split-second, Billy's realizes waistline is incidental.

"I'm still a spring chicken," he reminds the window-pane.

"Don't mix the darks with the whites today, Billy," Mrs. Hornpipe calls from the warmth of their bed.

Straw breaks Billy's reverie.

"Where are we playing today, Billy?"

IV

The monotony of recovery offends Billy. As if by rote, he ascends the south hill with Straw towards the statue of the writer. It is the time of pre-morning before the Billage wakes up. A light in a house plinks on here; a light in an apartment plinks on there; and one by one, each citizen concedes the sleepy arrival of dawn. He remembers all of these images so long ago during his commutes to work. It bothers Billy as he walks; the way graffiti continues to deface the Billage. He crests the hill with Straw. Billy passes along the main drag and the miracle mile. He notices the wonderful changes in the urban landscape: There are less for sale signs, less foreclosures and Billy sees the whole Billage under new management—vaguely international now, with less enclave and more community. Another burger-hut gives way to a shawarma shop. A bakery replaces a tattoo parlour. An empty Mortgage & Loan office morphs into a record store. Sure, there are still a thousand fast food joints but who fights city hall? Besides, like the mayor says, it's good for the cannabis industry or something.

Billy hears a kerfuffle. A kerfuffle is a lovesome noise. He gazes across the main drag and sees his friends in the other band. A snapping buckle creates a chain reaction of instrument cases closing. A bandleader in uniform with red stripes on the legs takes a pull on her cigarette. She flicks the butt, looks across the street and waves. Billy waves back.

It appears that each car in the parking lot feels safe now and knows that their doors will not get dented or dinged. Satisfied, Billy sucks air deep into his lungs and sighs. He stumblebums on and then pauses in front of the walk-in clinic.

"Billy. The industrial strength espresso machine is gone!" Straw cries.

"The burn barrel is still here," Billy replies.

A jangle of Straw's imaginary smartphone interrupts them.

Billy turns to Straw. "Not you too?"

"Wake up to technology," Straw says pointedly.

"Smartphones mark the death of the novel, Straw."

"Billy, why do you always need to fight the inevitable," Mrs. Hornpipe interjects.

It surprises Billy that he cannot get a word in edgewise.

"Will you fix my computer today?" he asks Mrs. Hornpipe.

Straw bows her head in homage, crinks her neck, takes the call and hands the smart phone over to Billy.

"It's Two-Bits, Billy."

"Where's my espresso machine, Kid?" Billy says.

"The mayor repossessed it, Billy Hornpipe. He just doesn't get Bit-coin and says we owe him two months' rent. Can you believe that? And that's after I found a pizza box and wrote .0000008 on it, right in front of him. I'm sorry, Billy. Listen, I *gotta* go make a million bucks. I don't have time for all this pension malarkey. I don't mean to be merciless. It's about the metaverse, Baby, and that's where I'm heading on a silver rocket. Thank you for bringing me into Stumblebum Waytes. Enjoy the Pink Moon."

"I thought we were in the metaverse," Billy replies.

"I left the valve trombone in the donation box at *Bin Around the Block*. Listen. I may be young and, on the go, but you remind me of an Old Me. Say goodbye to Straw for me."

"It is a pleasure to meet you," Billy replies and then hands the smartphone back to Straw.

Straw stokes the burn barrel but the smoke falters like an after-thought. The fire is indifferent and toys with the combustibles placed in it, satiated, like a thing over-fed.

Billy Hornpipe plops down on the iron bench beside Prometheus. He feels the presence of the writer against his thighs and ribs. As if by rote, he quietly assembles his shawm. He licks the reed and tightens it into place. The tip of Billy's tongue tells him the reed is not right. Straw flicks open the buckles of her black case. Tenderly, she lifts out her euphonium, finds the mouth piece and awaits Billy's cue.

"How about one more song and then I'll walk home with you?" Billy says wistfully.

"I could murder a coffee," Straw replies

Billy stands now. He pulls in a long tug of breath and raises his elbows. His chest expands under the gaze of a fading Pink Moon. Larger than life, Billy aligns his fingertips over the holes on his horn. He purses his lips like a prune and then sets the instrument down.

Straw follows his cue.

V

Billy rolls out of bed and regrets leaving the intimate warmth of Mrs. Hornpipe's body. He rises early, stops for an old man's *pee pee* and stumbles sleepily into the kitchen. He plugs in the kettle and makes an instant coffee like his father did before him. He knows that along with memory, DNA sequences inside him make involuntary choices about reality. Billy pauses and offers a prayer to his father, who, like a Cenotaph or a burn barrel or a statue, is a fixed thing inside him. He measures out a round spoonful of coffee, plops it into the mug and pours the hot water in. He stirs and prefers it black, like his mother. Billy acknowledges the acceptable addiction, bequeathed. He brings his mug to his nostrils and lets the steam take him. Billy craves the casual sensuality of morning routine.

"What are you going to do now that the espresso machine is gone?" Straw wonders.

"It was supposed to go," Billy smiles. "May I buy you a coffee over at the 24-hour joint?"

"It's not espresso, Billy."

"Nothing is," Billy replies wistfully.

Billy walks Straw over to the innerlit coffee shop behind the walk-in clinic. In the soft twilight, a patron sips alone at the counter, and then the room fills with murmur and the morning chatter of truck drivers. Billy sits across the table from Straw. She sits sleepily in repose. She props her elbows on the table between them and each arm forms an isosceles triangle with her mug at the apex. Billy admires the calculus and looks upon the last member of Stumblebum Waytes fondly.

Straw notices Billy's gaze and smiles.

"Where do we play today, Hand-wringer Hornpipe?

Billy guffaws.

"Why are you so mean this morning?"

"Because you are leaving," Straw says the way women perceive a change in affect, like breathing.

"How do you know?" he asks.

"Your fever is gone," Straw replies.

Billy feels his forehead and realizes she is right. He catches his image in the mirror behind the till. He sees his face is pink. He shifts to admire his waistline. Billy thinks perhaps, nobody sees him, but frankly everyone notices vain men. Mrs. Hornpipe puts on her look easily, but a man is a just a boy with a baseball cap on backwards and an imaginary pick-up truck. Billy pays for their coffee in real money and they exit the shop.

Billy sits on the iron bench. He feels the cold statue beside him: This Prometheus, who sits stoically and scribbles on his/her/our notepad. Billy watches the spray of Canada geese get loft above him and wobble in place atop firm stocks of iron. He thinks it is installation art at its finest. He marvels once again at the importance of permanence in the Billage of Blight; in a world where mirage plagues a reality that self-intelligence creates. Billy laughs when he spots another real-live goose. A straggler, she leaves the urban life for the corn, corn, corn of a better habitat.

Straw flicks open the buckles of her euphonium case, lifts the instrument and gently fits the mouthpiece. She moistens her lips and tests the keys with her right hand.

Billy is at a loss for words. Half-heartedly, he picks up his shawm and replaces the reed. He licks it and when it is supple, tightens it in the mouthpiece.

"The burn barrel just disappeared," Billy whispers.

"I have more at home," Straw laughs.

"Let's do Copeland's *Quiet City*, again," Billy says.

He reminisces now. Billy knows it is time to leave the comfort of his patterns but he lingers: He needs to linger, for a pattern tends to comfort: but when patterns weave together like snakes, change stops. Billy's bones ache. He wonders if this is what arthritis feels like. When he flexes his foot, his instep hurts.

Straw laughs the way a little girl laughs on a mountain.

"We'll improvise, Billy. This one's called *Quiet Billage*. On three. Come on: Let's go.… Two … three:"

Brass evokes an emotion that nothing else can. Billy listens and Straw becomes the melody. Somehow, she translates it from her heart into an adoration of all that is true and all that is good. The sound sweeps Billy triumphantly, the way music caresses perfectly the space it is given. Lost in time, present in the future, Billy almost misses his cue. He blows into his shawm: A thin string of notes lifts with melancholy between golden time signatures on a perfect stage made of brass.

Billy completely ignores the Pink Moon: He no longer turns: His dervish disappears: Each moon becomes irrelevant. Billy

Hornpipe feels the end of the song at his fingertips. He senses it is time to walk Straw home and say goodbye to Stumblebum Waytes.

Silence hugs the last note and then the beautiful sound of nothing echoes loud, pure and then whisks away. An early-bird breaks into song, then another: (Birds chirping): and soon, the commuting starts again: (Horns honking).

Straw purges the gob in the valves, breaks down the euphonium and places her instrument snugly in its black case. Billy removes his reed, examines it for wear and tear and decides to throw it out.

"Let's take a long walk along off a short pier, Billy," Straw laughs.

Together they head north, past the miracle mile and over the crest of the hill to descend to the four corners.

VI

As they descend, Billy notices that the graffiti disappears. He looks across the road and watches as more obscene script vanishes. He rubs his eyes and when he opens them, the Billage feels cleaner; fresh-as-a daisy after a shower. Billy notices cairns of stones replace spray-paint stains up and down the main drag. He remembers the Inuit name: Inuksuks. Billy pauses to touch an Inuksuk beside him. He feels hard ridges of uncut stone with his fingertips and marvels at the design of precise stacking. He knows the Inuksuk is a directional marker, a navigational aid that points the way to good fishing ground—thresholds between the spiritual world and the natural world. He loves deeper meanings to a fault.

Billy lets his gaze travel across the four corners, along the main drag and back again. An Inuksuk pops up at random intervals. At the four corners Billy notices a man on a golf cart. He lifts his wand skyward and waters a basket of flowers on a lamp post. The slap of overflow, patters beautifully upon the sidewalk below. It sounds like spring laughing.

"I think he is from Belize," Billy whispers.

"All the Inuksuks point south," Straw replies. "They all point to Prometheus."

"What could that possibly mean?" Billy laughs.

"An apex, Billy. An apex," Straw says and gets the calculus right.

Effortlessly, the man in the golf cart turns. Silently, he disappears around the corner by the fish market. Nothing new occupies the abandoned structure; it's just an old reality left to rot in the Billage.

"Some things take time," Billy whispers.

Billy crosses the four corners with Straw. An eighteen-wheeler approaches, growls its gears and prepares to make an illicit right turn at the light. The sound forces them to rush like killdeer, on tip-toe, with little quick-steps to make for safety at the curb. Billy looks over his shoulder and sees the rig completes its turn. It heads east towards Serenity Acres and the highway, beyond.

"Somebody should call a cop," Straw complains.

Billy stops in front of the window of the Obsessa. He looks inward. Darkness fills the interior. No longer aquatic, the space fills with dust and the ghosts of *Haversham Reno*. Billy rubs the glass. On a marble stand, an industrial strength espresso machine stands vigil in the corner. A white drop-cloth conceals its form but through a tear in the sheet Billy admires the copper marvel for what it is—this elegant rocket that reminds Billy of countless parties with Mrs. Hornpipe at the Italian club. He wiggles his toes, his in-steps ache but Billy anticipates he will dine on gnocchi and murder a plate of biscotti, next month.

"I need a shave," Billy says to a face in the window.

"It is important to tidy up," the window replies. "And you might want to lose those track pants, Bub."

Billy opens his hands at the waist and protests. "I'm retired," he says to the glass.

"Don't forget you have a pension," the glass replies.

A movement across the road reflects activity and Billy turns to observe. An older man, with long white hair and whiskers, enters the coffee franchise. He holds the door for a younger man, whose waistline is trim and his beard, even trimmer. The young man ignores the gesture, exits and strokes his smartphone. Billy remembers the urgency of the young; the energy of the young and the head-in-the-clouds selfishness of the young.

"How Millennial," Straw grumbles.

"There but for the future, go I," Billy replies in the kid's defense. "Besides, he cleans up good": (CC: free shipping).

Hail to the Chief rings stupidly on the cell, the young man pauses and bows in homage. He rushes off, around the corner by the bakery, to make millions on Bit-coin.

The light begins to change but there is no need for Billy to pick up the pace.

He passes the wet market patio and crosses the road to the pub where they finally get the curry right. Like box cars, a chain of vehicles shunts south, perennially en route to gridlock and conga lines.

"Walking is my new commute," Billy whispers, as if to reassure himself at twilight.

He crosses the bridge with Straw. He turns left at the long road that leads to the T-junction and then right, along the asphalt road; with the silver ribbon of riber on the left and the hills of cedar on the right. He spots a cone of lamplight at the junction.

"You don't have to go down their anymore, Billy," Straw whispers.

"I had a cardio-event," Billy confesses.

"It's okay, Honey-Bun. You're better now," Mrs. Hornpipe says. "Take Prometheus out for a walk: It's your turn and don't forget to pick up after him."

Straw's voice sounds distant. He turns and watches Straw walk down the laneway to her back yard. She leaves her Euphonium at the curb.

Billy calls out to her: "It is a pleasure to meet you. You were always the short Straw in our bunch!"

Billy lifts his face to feel the freshness of the morning. He peers up through a shady umbrella of tree limbs and sees the Pink Moon is long gone. He smells the sweet scent of wood stove in the air. Comfortable now in his own skin, Billy Hornpipe pats his waistline and cinches up his track pants. He places his shawm beside Straw's euphonium, pivots and walks along the long road towards the bridge and home.

A truck door slams. Billy turns and sees a garbage man remove trash from the curb. Satisfied that it is Monday, he returns to Mrs. Hornpipe and puts the water on for their coffee.

"Did you take your pills, Billy?"

"I did."

"Let's go out and get some fresh air."

"I know a bench where we can dream of the future."

"Does our future include painting the bathroom, Billy?"

"Yes, I believe it does."

ABOUT THE AUTHOR

Glenn Carley's published work includes *Polenta at Midnight: Tales of Gusto and Enchantment in North York* (2008); short stories in *Italian Canadians at Table* (2011); *Good Enough From Here* (2020); *Il Vagabondo: An Urban Opera* (2021); *Jimmy Crack Corn: A Novel in C Minor* (2022); *The Long Story of Mount Pester* and *The Long Story of Mount Pootzah* (both 2023), co-imagineered with and illustrated by his son, Nicholas Carley; and *The One about Stella: A Little Fish* (2024), written with his daughter, Adriana Carley. A resident of Bolton, Ontario, Carley is retired from the position of Chief Social Worker in a Toronto-area school board. He grandparents with his wife, Mary and together they grow.

www.ingramcontent.com/pod-product-compliance
Lightning Source LLC
Chambersburg PA
CBHW051233210726
48290CB00003B/935